God Is Dead

G

d

o

l

s

e

a

D

d

God Is Dead

Ron Currie, Jr.

Viking

VIKING

Published by the Penguin Group

Penguin Group (USA) Inc., 375 Hudson Street, New York, New York 10014, U.S.A. • Penguin Group (Canada), 90 Eglinton Avenue East, Suite 700, Toronto, Ontario, Canada M4P 2Y3 (a division of Pearson Penguin Canada Inc.) • Penguin Books Ltd, 80 Strand, London WC2R 0RL, England • Penguin Ireland, 25 St. Stephen's Green, Dublin 2, Ireland (a division of Penguin Books Ltd) • Penguin Books Australia Ltd, 250 Camberwell Road, Camberwell, Victoria 3124, Australia (a division of Pearson Australia Group Pty Ltd) • Penguin Books India Pvt Ltd, 11 Community Centre, Panchsheel Park, New Delhi – 110 017, India • Penguin Group (NZ), 67 Apollo Drive, Mairangi Bay, Auckland 1311, New Zealand (a division of Pearson New Zealand Ltd.) • Penguin Books (South Africa) (Pty) Ltd, 24 Sturdee Avenue, Rosebank, Johannesburg 2196, South Africa

Penguin Books Ltd, Registered Offices: 80 Strand, London WC2R 0RL, England

First published in 2007 by Viking Penguin, a member of Penguin Group (USA) Inc.

10   9   8   7   6   5   4   3   2   1

Copyright © Ron Currie, Jr., 2007
All rights reserved

The following stories were previously published in different form: "False Idols" appeared in *The Cincinnati Review;* "God Is Dead" in *The Sun;* "Interview" in *Alaska Quarterly Review;* and "Grace" in *Night Train.*

ISBN 978-0-670-03867-1

Printed in the United States of America
Designed by Carla Bolte • Set in Celeste

For my father, Ron Currie, Sr.

Contents

God Is Dead

Slaves, be obedient to them that are your masters according to the flesh, with fear and trembling, in singleness of your heart, as unto Christ.

—Ephesians 6:5

Disguised as a young Dinka woman, God came at dusk to a refugee camp in the North Darfur region of Sudan. He wore a flimsy green cotton dress, battered leather sandals, hoop earrings, and a length of black-and-white beads around his neck. Over his shoulder he carried a cloth sack which held a second dress, a bag of sorghum, and a plastic cup. He'd manifested a wound in the meat of his right calf, a jagged, festering gash upon which fed wriggling clumps of maggots. The purpose of the wound was twofold. First, it enabled him to blend in with the residents of the camp, many of whom bore injuries from the slashing machetes of Janjaweed raiding parties. Second, the intense burning ache helped to mitigate the guilt he felt at the lot of the refugees, over which he was, due to an implacable polytheistic bureaucracy, completely powerless.

Or nearly so. God did have the bag of sorghum, and the bag of sorghum was infinite, so that he was able to offer the sweet grain to others endlessly. For weeks he'd done this, following the path of the Lol River through scorched plains, giving away sorghum and asking if anyone knew a boy named Thomas Mawien. Most said no. Some, grateful for the food and eager to offer something in return, lied about knowing the boy, claimed to have seen him as recently as the day before, headed north, away from the fighting, or else southeast, and when God followed their directions he became hopelessly lost without the river to guide him. He wandered in wide circles, often coming upon the same boulder or stand of trees days after he'd first seen it. Denying himself the sorghum, he ate leaves, abuk roots, and on one occasion what was left of an ostrich carcass after it had been picked over by both people and hyenas.

He suffered under the sun he'd created. Sick with heat and cholera, he collapsed in a field of spindly yellow grass. His dress rode up immodestly, but he was paralyzed by dehydration, unable to even cover himself, and when two wild dogs came and began walking wide, hungry circles around him he could not move to drive them away.

Deliverance came in the form of the Janjaweed. The dogs heard their approach and bolted, but God, still paralyzed, could only lie in the grass and listen as the mass of horses and Land Rovers rumbled closer like some great and terrible machine, driving every living thing before it, shaking the earth as it passed. The Janjaweed saved him from the dogs, and his paralysis saved him from the Janjaweed; had he been able to rise and run they would have captured him easily, and seeing in him not the creator of this universe but rather a slender Dinka woman with a long, elegant neck and almond-shaped eyes, they would have raped him over and over until he died from the trauma.

But God remained hidden as the Janjaweed sped past all around him. Birds took to the sky; rodents scrambled for the safety of their burrows. Even the mosquitoes and cicadas fled. Bursts of semiautomatic fire sounded over the riot of diesel engines and galloping horses. A hoof, cracked and badly shoed, struck the ground inches from God's head. Still he could not move, did not make a sound.

And then, as quickly as they'd come, the Janjaweed were gone, leaving in their wake a silence so absolute even God had a difficult time believing it was real. He rested.

When he came to, it was light, and he found he could move again, if slowly and with great effort. He rose and followed the path of the Janjaweed, the trampled grass and burned huts and dead things of every description which led due north, and when he again reached the bank of the Lol he threw himself into the shallow water and drank greedily and tasted dirt and shit and did not care.

Early that afternoon, God entered the refugee camp along a rutted dirt path and approached the only people in sight, an elderly couple sitting together in the dust beneath a tamarind tree. Behind them the empty camp spread out in clusters of fragile huts made from thatch and torn plastic tarps.

"*Kudual,*" God said to the old couple in greeting. "Are you hungry? You look hungry."

The man sat hunched over and asleep, his bare legs folded beneath him like two bent sticks. The woman raised her eyes slowly and nodded yes. God offered the endless sorghum to her. With a hand as black and shriveled as a strip of jerked meat she reached in and removed a small amount, then held it to her chest with both hands, nodding modestly and muttering words of thanks.

"Take more," God said. "Please. There's plenty."

Without hesitating, the old woman did so. She placed the sorghum on the ground beside her, grasped and kissed God's hand (at which he, embarrassed and heartsick at the limits of his ability to help these people, demurred), then woke her husband with a rude jab of one bony elbow.

"Go find wood, and water for boiling," she said. "We have food."

With the deliberateness of someone who has learned never to feel too blessed, no matter how good the news, the man unfolded himself and stood up. God watched him recede into the empty camp.

"That man once owned five hundred head of cattle," the woman said. "Now look at him."

"Old woman, may I ask," God said, "do you know a boy named Thomas Mawien? Fifteen years old, but quite tall? He was taken as a slave by the Janjaweed many years ago. But he has escaped."

"I don't know him," the woman replied. "But that doesn't mean he's not here."

"It doesn't look like anyone's here," God said. "Did the Janjaweed attack?"

The woman laughed, revealing red, toothless gums. "No, not today," she said. "Today, with the big man here, we'll be safe."

"Which man is this?"

"The *ajak,* big man. Fat and pale like a mango. He comes to see us, from America. Wherever that is. Walks around, smiles, shakes hands."

From America. God knew then who this *ajak* was, and how he might be able to use him to find Thomas.

The woman continued. "Tomorrow he goes home"—she made a motion with her hand like a plane lifting into the air— "and the Janjaweed come back."

"Where is he now?" God asked.

"On the west side of the camp," the woman said. "That's why you don't see anyone. They're all following him around out there, singing and dancing like fools."

▪

Colin Powell hid from an angry sun in the air-conditioned interior of his Chevrolet Suburban. Head down, he spoke quietly into a satellite telephone. A senior State Department official sat on the leather bench seat opposite him, holding Powell's linen Ralph Lauren jacket across his lap. Outside, the Secret Service attachment had formed a tight perimeter around the Suburban. To a man they wore black boots, khaki pants and vests, mirrored sunglasses, and thigh holsters with SIG-Sauer P229 pistols. Each brandished a Heckler & Koch MP5 submachine gun. The agents scanned the singing, ululating crowd of Dinka refugees, exchanged information (and the occasional one-liner) via tiny earpieces, and maintained a robotic, perspiration-free command presence despite the 95-degree heat.

With a curse, Powell turned off the telephone. "Tell me something," he said to the official. "Why do I always end up relaying messages through the lowliest goddamn sub-assistant-deputy aides in the White House? Why, in almost four years, have I spoken directly to that redneck son of a bitch only *three times*? And two of those times were at fucking *Christmas* parties?"

"I don't know, sir," the official said. "Maybe that gaffe you made in the *Post* last February? But listen, we should go over our keywords for tonight's press conference—"

"I'll tell you why," Powell said. "Because I'm black."

The official, uncertain, said, "Well, maybe, sir."

"The same reason I got this job in the first place," Powell continued. "Because I'm black. Ain't that a bitch, huh? I get the job because I'm black, and my boss won't talk to me because I'm black."

"If I may speak frankly, sir," the official said, "I'm not sure *black* is the word I'd use to describe you."

Powell deployed a fierce, wide-eyed gaze, one he'd perfected through hundreds of hours of viewing and reviewing Samuel Jackson movies. "Oh no?" he said.

The official, realizing he'd stepped directly into the metaphorical pile of dung, tried to backtrack. "Well, of course, I mean, ethnologically speaking, you're black. Sir. Of course. I was thinking more of your *appearance,* a sort of benign, nonthreatening, *ashy* tone which—"

"I'm black as night, motherfucker!" With a sweep of his hand, Powell indicated the throng of Dinka surrounding the Suburban. "Those people out there," he said, "are my brothers and sisters. My *family.*"

"Of course they are, sir," the official said. "Sorry, sir."

"Apology accepted. Bitch-ass."

"Back to the keywords for tonight, sir. If we may."

"Lay it on me."

"Okay, so we're talking about the Sudanese government and our attitude toward them. Keywords for our attitude, as regards the humanitarian situation here, include, but are not limited to: 'steady,' 'demand,' 'firm,' 'control the Janjaweed,' 'do what's right,' and 'solution.'"

"Got it," Powell said.

"Keywords for the Sudanese government include, but are not limited to: 'denial,' 'avoidance,' 'responsibility,' 'militarism,' 'racism,' and—here's your ace in the hole, sir—'obfuscate.'"

"The fuck does that mean?"

"To obscure or confuse. Ties directly into 'denial' and 'avoidance.' Trust me, sir, it'll bring the house down."

"If you say so," Powell said. "Okay. I'll go out and do my little soft-shoe routine. Make it look like that hillbilly actually gives a shit what's going on here."

There was a sudden commotion outside. Powell looked up and saw two agents restraining what was surely the most beautiful young black woman he had ever seen. The agents struggled to keep the woman away from the Suburban. One grasped the green fabric of her dress, while the other applied a choke hold and issued a firm textbook directive for her to cease and desist. The woman was calling to Powell through the window's reflective, bulletproof, blast-resistant glass. A third agent, pistol drawn and pointed at the woman's head, moved to join the fray.

Powell threw open the door of the Suburban to a hammer stroke of dry heat. "What's wrong with you men?" he hollered. "Let her go!"

The agent choking the woman loosened his grip. "She rushed the vehicle, Mr. Secretary," he said.

With a fierce gesture, Powell called the agent over to him. "Perhaps you failed to notice the hundred or so cameras here," he whispered through clenched teeth. "Perhaps you also failed to notice that this woman is wounded. Perhaps, finally, you failed to notice that she speaks perfect, unaccented English, and doesn't that strike you as a bit odd in this place, you dumb cracker?"

"Yes, Mr. Secretary, I suppose it does."

"Then let her go, and let her speak."

The agent turned and motioned to his colleagues, who stepped aside. The woman lifted her cloth sack from where it had fallen in the dirt, straightened her dress, and approached the Suburban.

Powell smiled. "What can I do for you, sugar?"

"Mr. Secretary," the woman said, her large eyes brimming with tears, "I need your help."

■

"We are anxious to see the end of *militarism*," Powell said. "We are anxious to see the *Janjaweed brought under control* and disbanded so people can leave the camps in safety and go back to their homes."

In front of the cameras, under a large canvas tent erected for the press conference, God sat to Powell's immediate right. To Powell's left the Sudanese foreign minister, Mustafa Osman Ismail, tried without success to summon a smile to his face. The senior State Department official stood just out of view of the cameras, hanging on Powell's every word.

"I've delivered a *steady* message to Mr. Ismail that the violence must be addressed," Powell said to the assembled reporters. "The *solution* has to rest with the government *doing what's right*."

He turned to Ismail, who finally managed the smile of benevolence and cooperation he'd been after by envisioning Powell's head atop a pike.

"To that end, in a show of good faith, Mr. Ismail has agreed to assist in locating Thomas Mawien, who was abducted by the Janjaweed and forced into slavery a decade ago, and whose sister Sora, seated here with me, asked for our help in finding her brother. For my part, I've promised Sora that I will not leave Darfur until she and Thomas are reunited. So we'll all be sticking around a little longer than we'd thought."

The official, whose left eyelid had begun to twitch when Powell wandered further and further off-message, now performed a spasmodic little dance as he fought the impulse to rush in and swat the cluster of microphones off the table.

"As we speak, units of the Sudan People's Liberation Army are scouring the region for Thomas. Once he is returned to his sister in good condition, then, and only then, can we be assured that the Sudan government is not merely continuing its campaign of *denial* and *avoidance.* Only then can we be assured they are no longer trying to *obfuscate* and avoid any consequences.

"Thank you," Powell said, rising from his seat. "That's all for now." The mass of reporters rose with him, waving their hands and clamoring as one attention-starved organism. The official rushed in, screaming, "No questions! No questions!" Powell put an arm around God, held the pose for several seconds while the cameras flashed, then turned and offered his hand to Ismail. For a moment Ismail merely stood and regarded the hand as one regards a dead squirrel or a fresh pile of dog feces, but gave it a limp, spiteful shake when Powell fixed him with the Samuel Jackson stare. Then, flanked by his entourage, he turned and strode out of the tent.

The official turned to Powell as the Secret Service agents began herding reporters out into the arid night. "Due respect, sir," he said, "are you insane? We're scheduled to be in Indonesia tomorrow. Sir, it's *already* tomorrow in Indonesia."

"Indonesia isn't going anywhere," Powell told him.

"Besides which," the official said, "besides which, sir, and forgive me if I'm out of line here, but our function is not to *order* foreign governments around. Our function is to *persuade* and *convince.*"

"Fuck that," Powell said. "I'm a general, don't forget. And generals give orders. Like I'm giving you an order right now: Leave me alone."

The official's satellite telephone rang, a shrill, angry sound. He clawed at his jacket, found the phone, and clutched it to his ear with both hands.

"Yes?" His face blanched. "Yes, sir . . . sir, I don't know . . . this is as much a surprise to . . . I have no idea why the secretary has turned off his telephone . . . sir, let me . . . let me assure you that I remain a faithful servant of the admin . . . sir, perhaps you'd like to speak with . . . yessir, he's right here."

The official thrust the phone at Powell. "It's the president."

Powell waved him away. "Take a message," he said.

■

The aide seated next to Mustafa Osman Ismail in the back of the Land Rover hadn't noticed that morning how rough the road was between the refugee camp and El Fasher, where they were staying during the Americans' visit. Tonight, though, as they drove across dried mud plains under the silver crescent of a new moon, it seemed the minute vibration of every crack and pebble was amplified a thousandfold in the freshly broken bones of his forearm.

The young aide had learned, in the few seconds it took for Ismail to coolly and expertly snap his right radius into two distinct pieces, a few lessons:

1. Ismail's famous smile was the equivalent of a smile on a shark.
2. Ismail's slender build belied tremendous physical strength.
3. It was not wise to speak to Ismail when he'd just been humiliated by a foreign diplomat, especially one from America.

Pain instructs. The aide had assimilated these lessons so completely that he dared not make a sound now. Even as the vehicle rattled and bucked, rubbing raw jagged bone on bone, he didn't so much as whimper.

Ismail himself finally broke the agonized silence.

"I want you to call Rahman," he said to the aide. "Tell him his men have until tomorrow noon to find this boy."

The aide considered asking if he should issue a specific threat along with the order, but then decided, based on his recent experience, that a grave threat indeed was probably implicit.

"Yes, Doctor," he said through gritted teeth.

"We'll deliver the boy to Powell," Ismail said. "He will be satisfied, and he will go away. But the moment the wheels of his plane leave the runway, I'll take the leash off the Janjaweed. And I won't put it back on until every Dinka in that camp is dead."

"I've never questioned any of my decisions," Colin Powell told God. "Not as a kid, not in Vietnam, not as chairman of the Joint Chiefs. Plenty of opportunities to wonder if I was doing the right thing. Sixty-seven years, a skyrocket of a career—I never once doubted any decision I made. Then, on the plane here, I get a phone call—a simple phone call, lasted maybe three minutes—and suddenly I'm certain, absolutely *certain,* that every choice I made before today was wrong."

Powell sat cross-legged on the dirt floor of the conference tent. God lay on a cot Powell had ordered brought in after telling the senior State Department official they would not be returning to the hotel in El Fasher. Outside, beyond the ring of Secret Service agents standing guard, they could hear the quiet conversations of Dinka families, the pop and hiss of campfires, the sigh of a steady plains wind.

"Except for marrying Alma," Powell said. "That was the right decision. But other than that."

Despite an acute awareness of his responsibility for the circumstances that had led to Powell's crisis of confidence, God was exhausted, sick with both guilt and a blood infection from the gash on his leg, and he found himself wishing Powell would be quiet so he could sleep.

Still, the guilt won out, and God asked, "Who was the phone call from?"

Powell shifted his bulk and sighed. "A woman named Rita, who I knew a long time ago, when we were children. Her brother Keith and I were friends. Keith was killed, and I was the only person who knew what had happened. But I never told."

For a moment neither of them spoke.

"Rita's at a retirement home in South Carolina now, dying of liver cancer," Powell said.

"Did you tell her?" God asked.

"Yes."

"And how do you feel now?"

Powell looked up. "Terrible," he said.

"I'm sure Rita is grateful," God said. "To finally know what became of her brother."

"I ask myself, finally," Powell continued, "how does a man become the first black assistant to the president for national security affairs? How does a man become the first black chairman of the Joint Chiefs? How does a man become the first black secretary of state? And then I answer myself: by behaving, in every possible manner, like a white man."

God said nothing. Instead he did what he always did, all he was allowed to do: sympathize, sympathize.

"The highest-ranking, most powerful house nigger in history," Powell said. "That's me."

Later that night, however—after the fires had burned themselves down and filled the air with the thick honeyed scent of smoldering cinders, after the conversations had faded one by one and were replaced by the gentle sound of forty thousand people dreaming the same dream under a sequined sky, after God had gone into a fevered sleep and even a few of the Secret Service agents had begun to flag and slump outside the tent— Powell had to admit that he'd committed political suicide today not just for the sake of a belated racial pride, but for something simpler and more tangible: a chance at redemption.

Because it had not been gratitude that he'd heard in Rita's voice. No. What had been converted from sound into electrical signals, traveled through thousands of miles of telephone wire, uplinked and bounced from one satellite to another, then transmitted to his telephone and converted back into sound was pure, unalloyed grief. Fresh grief at Keith's death, yes, but more than that, the grief of finding out too late for things to be set right.

And now, here was this strange, beautiful girl, this Sora,

who wanted nothing but to find her brother. Powell, at least for the time being, had the power to help her do that. And he'd be damned if he wasn't going to try.

■

Weeks later the senior State Department official (who had never been well liked precisely because his need to be liked was so transparently desperate) would find himself invited to every cocktail party and cigar lounge bull session in the Beltway, and he would relate, time and again, his insider's version of the ex-secretary of state's meltdown.

"It was a sudden, out-of-the-blue thing," he told a group of young State Department attorneys during happy hour at the Hawk and Dove. By now he was so well rehearsed that he didn't need to think about what he was saying, and could simply enjoy the undivided attention of all these people (and in particular that of one willowy blonde who was still young enough to chain-smoke with listless indifference and who, he would discover later that night, bore a vaguely Pentagon-shaped birthmark behind her left knee). "It started without warning on the flight to Sudan. Powell got a call from some old bat he'd grown up with. The whole thing started," the official said, "with a phone call."

The group let out a collective groan of disbelief. Several took advantage of this break in the narrative to sip their microbrews and cosmopolitans.

"How in the world did she get through on a secure line?" the blonde asked.

"Powell's wife pushed the call through," the official said. "Apparently this woman called his home first."

Another groan. Glasses clinked. Cigarettes flared.

"Give me a break," someone said.

The official raised his eyebrows and shrugged.

A lawyer whose vulpine features seemed vaguely familiar to the official chimed in. "You're trying to tell us that the man who could have snapped his fingers and been the first black President was derailed by a call from his childhood sweetheart?"

The official smiled. "I'm trying to tell you that the day after he took that call was the first time he called me a no-good honky motherfucker. But certainly not the last."

∎

Dawn broke torrid and clear over the camp and found God hunched in the entryway of the conference tent, wrapped in a military-issue wool blanket. Infection hummed in his blood. Shivering with fever, he watched as women dressed in brilliant reds and greens shuttled water in plastic buckets atop their heads. Others sat in a food queue that stretched out of sight into the dense congregation of lean-tos. These women stirred and rose to their feet as Powell appeared, flanked by the senior State Department official and two Secret Service agents. A wave of chanting and clapping followed Powell as he approached the conference tent. God could see he was smiling.

"Sora," he said, clasping God's hands in his own. "They found Thomas."

Practically underfoot, two young boys giggled as they crouched and bathed one another with water from a dented tin can marked BEANS.

Powell gave God's hands an urgent squeeze. "Sora? They found your brother. They're on their way here."

Over Powell's shoulder God saw a scrawny cow being led by a teenage girl. The cow struggled to keep pace. Its ribs strained the skin with each step. Greenish foam blossomed at its nostrils, and its udder dangled like an empty glove. As God watched, the cow took half a step forward, staggered back, and died on its feet. For a moment it remained standing. Then it began to collapse with terrible slowness, as if it remembered gravity but did not agree with it. The front legs folded at the knee, and the rear end listed to one side, dragging the rest of the body down into the dust.

In an instant flies swarmed around its mouth and eyes. The girl stared at the carcass with the stunned indifference of a catatonic. Over the chanting of the women in the food queue and the giggling of the boys rose a high, steady sound, a single note of distilled grief which God knew came from the girl, but even as she threw herself down and wrapped her arms around the dead animal her face remained still and expressionless.

The giggling and chanting and splashing and clapping went on and on. God felt with certainty and relief that he, too, was dying.

"Sora," Powell said. The smile was gone; he peered into God's face with concern. "You should lie down. Thomas will be here soon."

God allowed himself to be led back into the tent by the Secret Service agents. They eased him onto the cot and draped another blanket over him.

Powell's telephone rang from within his rumpled suit. "I want you to find someone from the medical tent," he told an agent as he searched his pockets for the phone. "Get them in here as soon as possible."

Powell lifted the phone to his ear and turned away. "Yes," he said. There was a pause. "Well I'm afraid you can't fire me. Because I quit."

■

"I must be dumb as a brick," Powell said. He'd left the tent to avoid upsetting Sora and now strode angrily and without direction through the camp, shouting into the telephone, trailed by a Secret Service agent and a steadily growing crowd of Dinka admirers. "Because I actually thought your stupid ass might be capable of seeing that in this instance the right thing to do is also the smart thing to do, politically speaking."

Pause.

"I said *stupid ass*."

Pause.

"Smart politically because if you got behind what I'm doing here people would see a president transcending the rhetoric of diplomacy and *acting* for once. Doing something good, no matter how small."

Pause.

"Don't give me *delicate and complicated*. What am I, some bright-eyed Georgetown undergrad, gonna change the world? It's only delicate and complicated because we make it delicate and complicated."

Pause.

"What happened to me? You want to know *what happened* to me?"

Pause.

"All right. Let me give you a hypothetical. Pay attention, because there will be a quiz at the end."

Pause.

"Let's say you're a black kid growing up in the Bronx. Imagine it's the hottest summer you've seen in your eight years, and the war's over and everyone in the neighborhood has lost their job because all the white men have come back from Europe and the Pacific looking for work themselves. And so everyone's packed in on everyone else, every day, in the heat. Then say someone's had enough and they pick up a rock and break a window. Who knows why? Maybe they're anarchists; maybe they're union agitators; maybe they're just bored. For a week after that you smell tear gas every morning when you wake up. A third of the buildings on your block burn to the ground.

"Now imagine your mother, who saw much worse than this where she's from and maybe isn't as worried as she should be, sends you to the store. She sends you with an older boy named Keith who lives in your building. Keith is fourteen and supposed to keep you out of trouble. Except there's nothing but a scorched foundation where the store used to be, so you have to walk sixteen blocks north, all the way to Cab's Grocery. On your way back the milk and oranges are getting heavy and Keith wants to take a shortcut. So you duck down an alley and Keith tells you to climb this chain-link fence and he'll pass you the food and you'll cut through this backyard except you only get halfway up the fence before a cop grabs you by the seat of your pants and pulls you off.

"The cop slams you on the pavement and presses his boot on your neck. You smell dirt and mink oil. Pebbles bite the side of your face. You try to turn your head but the boot presses harder and the cop says, *Just take it easy, boyo.*

"A second cop is talking to Keith. *What are you jigs up to? You going to break into this place?* And Keith, who is always getting into fights he can't win because his mouth is a lot tougher than his fists, says *Fuck you.* Then you hear a sound like someone hitting a side of beef with a baseball bat, over and over, and Keith is crying, then screaming, then silent.

"*Jesus Christ,* says the cop whose boot is on your neck.

"You're jerked to your feet and thrown face-first against the fence. The second cop presses against you from behind. His body is trembling. He hooks his fingers through the fence and leans close and whispers in your ear. *Not a word to anyone, you fucking niglet.* His breath is hot and moist on your cheek, and stinks like onions.

"They let you go. You run all the way home, and your mother wants to know what happened, what's wrong, where's Keith, where's the food. But you don't tell. Your father returns from work and asks you the same questions, and you don't tell. A few days later the police come and sit at the kitchen table and drink your mother's coffee and ask the same questions, but their voices are all too terribly familiar, and you don't tell.

"You keep this secret your whole life. You do such a good job of keeping it that after a while it seems like maybe it didn't happen at all, maybe it was a story someone else told you, or maybe just a dream.

"Half a century later, you're flying to Senegal on a diplomatic mission one night, and you can't sleep. You watch a movie. The movie gets you to thinking about how things haven't changed a bit, despite the fact that you're the most powerful black man in the history of the most powerful nation on earth. You haven't thought about Keith for years, but you do now, and it all comes back to you as real as if it happened yesterday—the wet smack of the nightstick on his skull, the smell of oranges crushed on hot pavement. Real. It happened. It was not a dream.

"And then you realize you're the only black person on this plane."

Pause.

"How would you feel? How would you talk? How would you behave, you silver-spoon master-of-the-universe motherfucker?"

Pause.

"Hypothetically speaking?"

■

A motorcade of five army jeeps and one late-model Land Rover tore into the refugee camp at noon, kicking up dust and scattering children. Powell watched as the procession ground to a halt in front of the conference tent. Angry-looking men in dirty fatigues spilled from the jeeps, assault rifles in hand. Ismail emerged from the Land Rover, followed by his aide (who wore a clumsy makeshift splint on his right forearm), and finally a tall but crookbacked boy dressed only in tattered shorts and sandals.

The three approached Powell. Ismail motioned to the boy. "Introduce yourself," he said.

"I am Thomas Mawien," the boy said in belabored English. He looked at Ismail, then cast his eyes to the ground. "The brother of Sora."

"I know who you are, son." Powell hugged the boy, then turned to lead him into the tent.

"You are satisfied, Mr. Powell?" Ismail called after them.

"Just wait here," Powell said.

Inside was dark and cool. Motes of sand drifted on the air, illuminated by a shaft of sunlight from the open entryway. A doctor stood beside God's cot, adjusting the flow of an IV drip.

"Sora," Powell said. "Thomas is here."

God opened his eyes, blinked a few times, coughed weakly.

Powell pulled the doctor aside. "How long will the treatment take?" he asked. "We have to leave as soon as we can. Today."

"It is not possible," the doctor told him. "She needs three or four rounds of antibiotics. Much too sick to travel. Maybe in a week or two, with improvement. But right now, no."

God sat up and struggled to focus on the figure at the foot of the cot, thinking that his eyes, blurred by fever, were misleading him. He took a long look while the boy shifted from foot to foot, unsure what to do.

"You are not Thomas," he said finally, in Arabic.

"I am," the boy said without much conviction.

"No. Your face is similar, and you are tall like him. But you're not Thomas."

The boy wrung his hands. "Please," he said.

"The men who brought you here. Did they tell you to say you were my brother?"

"Yes."

"But you're not. You're not Thomas."

The boy looked toward Powell and the doctor. "No."

"Did they threaten you? The soldiers?"

"Yes."

God regarded him for a moment, then said, "Turn around slowly so I can look at you."

The boy did as he was told. His wrists, ankles, and neck all bore the banded scars left by rawhide straps when they stay tied too tight for too long. His back, twisted by work and malnutrition, was crisscrossed with the rougher raised scars of the whip.

"Where do you come from?" God asked.

"Until this morning I tended goats for a man named Hamid."

"And before that? Who were you before?"

"I don't know," the boy said. "I've forgotten."

Guilt gathered in God's throat and formed a lump there. He realized with sudden certainty that this boy, or any of the people in the camp—the men suddenly alone in their old age, the young women with disappeared husbands and hungry children— were as deserving as Thomas of his apology, would serve just as well as the altar for him to confess his sins of omission and beg forgiveness. God slid from the cot and stooped on his knees before the boy, like a Muslim at prayer. The unfamiliar twinge of tears stung his eyes, and he was about to speak when the boy crouched and put a hand on his shoulder.

"Please," the boy said, "get on your feet." He cast frightened glances around the tent, as if expecting Ismail and the soldiers to appear at any moment.

God looked up. "I'm sorry," he said.

"Please," the boy said again, tugging urgently at the shoulder of God's dress. "If you show weakness, it only makes them angry."

∎

Several hours after Powell departed, taking the boy with him and promising to return, God removed the IV from his arm and staggered outside to seek relief from the stale air inside the tent. He gazed out toward the eastern horizon and spotted the first plane, a tiny blemish on the sky. Soon it was joined by a dozen more, all drifting around one another in tight slow circles like a swarm of tsetse flies.

Most of the camp's inhabitants had taken shelter in their

lean-tos or under tamarinds to wait out the hottest part of the day, but as news spread of the odd spots in the distance, people began to stir. Mothers looked at the sky as though checking the weather, then roused the children and gathered their belongings as an ominous wall of dust formed in the east and the planes drew nearer, flying now in attack formation.

God crouched on his haunches, pulled the blanket tight around his shoulders, and waited. The Dinka scrambled with mounting urgency. They rushed to the well for a last drink of water and untethered the few goats and donkeys in their possession. One woman lost a sandal in her haste, but rather than stop to remove the other she hobbled as fast as she could, clutching the wrist of her young daughter and pulling her along. Those who were late in rising simply got to their feet and ran, leaving behind everything they owned.

Sunlight glinted off the planes' wingtips. From the wall of dust, trailing slightly behind the planes, God heard the first faint bursts of automatic gunfire. The ground began to tremble minutely.

Time and again the people still in the camp, realizing they were now trapped, called to God in a hundred different dialects. He laughed and cried at once. He had so many names, yet could not answer to any of them.

The planes flashed overhead. They pitched forward and dropped their payloads. God did not look up. He watched the dust storm, where great black horses materialized like wraiths, their coats slick with foam, their nostrils angry and flared. The men astride these horses swung wicked blades and took aim with their rifles. Their faces were hidden in checked scarves. The bombs whistled down, down. The ground shook. God closed his eyes and wished for someone he could pray to.

The Bridge

There will be signs in the sun, moon, and stars.

—Luke 21:25

Dani Kitchen drove the usual route home to her mother's, through the overgrown fields that stretched to the horizon on either side of Route 201. The sun rode fat and high even in late afternoon, and the two-lane blacktop in the distance shimmered like spilled gasoline. Tall grass, reeds, and cattails bowed in a mellow breeze, interspersed with strawberry patches and plots of juvenile corn, which was now only waist-high but by the end of August, when she was gone from here and starting school in Chapel Hill, would stand eight or ten feet tall.

For once Dani was not in a hurry, and actually stayed under the speed limit at a leisurely fifty miles per hour. Wind from the open window blew her hair into a tangled mess. A blond swatch lapped at her cheek, then found purchase in the moisture at the corner of her mouth and clung there. Rather than pull the strand out and tuck it behind her ear, Dani laughed and gathered the hair with her tongue, sucked on it, tasting the slight bitterness of shampoo that hadn't quite rinsed out of the ends that morning.

In the backseat of her Grand Am, in a crumpled pile, sat her shiny white graduation cap and gown. Her diploma had fallen to the floor and lay, already forgotten, among the Pepsi cans, an overdue movie rental, crusts of dirt left over from the previous winter.

She passed the Shores' farm, where she picked up meat for her mother twice a month—Carol, the old man, sold steaks and freezer pigs, white cheese and sandwich ham right out of his barn. All slaughtered, cut, cured, and decanted on the premises. He'd been at it since he was a boy, had inherited the farm from his father, and now was in his mid-seventies. Rumor was that he might be selling out to a developer who wanted to turn his pastures into a Wal-Mart. The place smelled like shit and murder, but Dani liked it there, liked Carol's slow, jokey personality, how he sort of was the farm instead of just the guy who ran it. Dani called hello to the cows, honked the car horn at them, but they took no notice of her, just went on with the slow, ponderous business of grazing.

She laughed again and drove on.

With one hand she tapped out a beat on the steering wheel. With the other she reached for the pack of cigarettes in the console between the bucket seats. She lit one and inhaled deeply and without guilt, for Dani was a girl (a woman, she reminded herself, she needed to begin thinking of herself as a woman, a college woman, and perhaps along the same line of thought it was time to consider referring to herself, and asking others to refer to her, by her full name) who believed, deep down where she held her strongest and most intuitive convictions, that nothing bad would ever happen to her. She was smart enough to know that this made her not terribly unlike every other eighteen-year-old who had ever driven too fast or taken up smoking. Still, there it was—she believed in her clear skin, her white teeth, her strong slender legs. The world hadn't yet given her reason to doubt them, and until it did she was invulnerable, and behaved accordingly, and didn't really give it a whole hell of a lot of thought one way or the other.

A week ago, for example, while in the damp and still somewhat awkward clutches of sex, she could feel Ben's shoulders tighten and tremble as he neared his orgasm, and he slowed down and held off and said in her ear, "I want to do it inside you."

Dani shifted her body underneath him and said, as if she didn't know, "Do what?"

Embarrassed, bashful as always, Ben tucked his chin against his chest. "You know."

"Yeah," she said. She lifted his chin with one hand, forcing him to meet her eyes. "But I want to hear you say it."

"No," Ben said. "Never mind."

Touched by the boy's shyness, Dani felt her heart swell with an affection that was more maternal than erotic, and she said, "Oh, Ben, you do whatever you want to, baby."

And, thus encouraged, he did. Dani's mother would have called this *careless,* a word she often used to describe her daughter's behavior. But Dani didn't worry. She knew things, and she wasn't going to end up like her mother, saddled with a baby and on her own before her eighteenth birthday. Even in the midst of Ben's orgasm, she could feel the muscles inside her working, forcing him out, gently but firmly. When he finished and collapsed on top of her she pushed him off, her lips brushing his forehead, and stood to go to the bathroom, and before she even placed her hand on the toilet paper roll the fluid was running out of her and down the inside of her thigh, turning cold, impotent, harmless—just a little mess to wipe up and be done with.

When she came back she did not lie down, but instead sat on the edge of the bed and folded one leg up underneath her butt. Ben stroked her back with his fingertips. He mentioned something about a bonfire, a party up at the water tower, but Dani wasn't listening; her mind had wandered to thoughts of the coming fall, moving to North Carolina for college, her life beyond and after this place, and she could not think of a single thing here that she would cry for.

And while her girlfriends would have spent the next few days waiting for the worst, hoping for the twinge and flow that would let them know they had gotten away with their carelessness, Dani went about the business of the last week of high school without a moment's worry. She attended marching practice and the senior talent show. She filled out her last will and testament for the *Panther Press,* and got drunk and kissed someone who was not Ben at Matt Bouchard's senior campout. And when her period came she hardly noticed at all.

Dani turned off the pavement onto a fire access road, heading for the first of two stops she would make to cap off this day of ritualized symbolic transition. The gravel road wound along a downward slope toward McGrath Pond, made slightly steeper and more treacherous each year by the erosive flow of spring runoff. At several spots the road turned sharply, weaving between trees and rough-hewn granite boulders, and Dani pressed the brake most of the way down. After half a mile the trees parted and the pond came suddenly into view, its water the color of a propane flame. Modest whitecaps, kicked up by the breeze, dotted the pond's surface. Dani pulled into a turnoff near the public boat landing and put the car in park.

She got out, came around to the back, and unlocked the trunk. It sprang open with a pop, and she removed a plastic grocery bag, heavy with mementos, then closed the trunk again.

To the left of the boat landing, under a stand of slender white birches, was a makeshift and illegal fire pit ringed with blackened rocks. The rocks were piled on one another in a semicircle. In the pit were the remains of a fire from who knew how long ago—a bed of ash, sodden and muddy from the previous night's rain, on top of which lay half-burned sticks of wood, a few scorched beer cans, and the melted ruins of a pair of sneakers. Dani reached into the bag and removed a squeeze-tin of lighter fluid, then upended the bag and watched the bits and pieces of her life up to this point fall into the pit. Without hesitation or malice—without much feeling at all, really, except for the warm and constant sense of anticipation she'd felt all day long—she squirted half the tin onto the photographs and baby shoes and certificates of achievement, struck a match, and tossed it on the pile.

But this wasn't the movies; the match went out before it hit the fluid. Dani struck another. She cupped the delicate flame with one hand, kneeled, and touched the matchhead to the fur of a stuffed panda bear. The lighter fluid caught instantly, and she jumped back as the entire pile went up.

Dani lit a cigarette and watched her things burn, glancing occasionally out on the pond, where two loons swimming alongside one another dove in sync, disappearing seamlessly beneath the water. She was reminded of the time when, as a little kid, she'd seen a man in a speedboat chase a loon around this same pond. For some reason the bird had been unable to fly—perhaps she had a broken wing. But she'd seen the boat coming and ducked under the water, resurfacing a minute or two later fifty yards away. The man went after her again, and again the loon dove. Dani remembered the noise of the engine, how it idled with a predatory grumble as the man waited for the bird to surface, then roared when she came up for air, the sound carrying across the water to where Dani and her mother lay sunbathing. She remembered the glinting diamond of sunlight from the chrome light fixture on the bow of the boat, bearing down again and again on the harried bird. This went on for an hour, with the loon tiring, spending less and less time underwater, moving shorter and shorter distances from the boat before resurfacing, until finally she came up one last time, and the man gunned the outboard, and the bird was too tired to dive again, and that was the end of her.

It was the only time Dani could ever remember crying, as a kid. *Why, Mama?* she'd howled over and over, and her mother, gazing dry-eyed out at the man in his boat, shook her head a little and said, *I don't know, hon. Some men are just that way.* And Dani couldn't understand, still did not understand why her mother didn't shed even one tear for the bird, or for her daughter's grief.

This, though—the willful destruction of the keepsakes of her young life—her mother would shed a tear or two over this, Dani knew. The thought gave her no pleasure; it was something she had to do for herself, and how it might affect anyone else really didn't figure into it. Besides, her mother would never understand that for Dani, this was a joyous act, a sloughing off of things old and worn and useless—her way of giving the future a big welcoming hug.

But something was missing. She wanted to wake up tomorrow completely new and unfettered, and somehow the things she'd set ablaze, most of which were now burned down to embers and ash, weren't enough. So she walked back to the car and took the cap and gown and diploma from the backseat. Again without hesitation, she tossed them on the fire. The cap and gown disintegrated, casting off a tremendous chemical stench. The diploma, in its faux-leather binding, took longer to burn. Dani poked at it with a stick. She knew that her mother would do more than cry over her burning the diploma, would, in fact, curse her daughter for it, having been unable to finish high school herself after getting pregnant with Dani. Her mother considered the diploma an end in itself, while for Dani it was just a means to a greater end—that of college, and all the doors it would open. The piece of paper itself held no real meaning for her, although she did put great stock in symbols and symbolism, signs and premonitions.

This day, for example—this perfect, beautiful day. The bright sunlight and warm breeze, the cows and their lazy grazing, the matched pair of loons—all of it an unmistakable sign of something good. Dani rarely if ever needed cheering up, but she welcomed it all the same.

Just as the diploma burned down to flaky glowing ash, the loons emerged again from the pond's depths. Bobbing among the waves, they shook themselves dry, head to tail, then unfolded their wings and began to skim across the surface of the pond, picking up speed, lifting themselves until just their thin black feet still skittered through the water. They lifted their feet like the landing gear on a jetliner, tucking them into their downy underbellies, then rose steeply and made a wide turn overhead, disappearing over the tree line.

Watching the birds, Dani thought again about just leaving for North Carolina immediately. Why not? Why stick around here, working at the House of Pancakes all summer long, when she could leave right away and be in Chapel Hill, with a new apartment and new friends, well before the fall semester started? It was the sort of impulse, Dani knew, that would give her girl-friends hives, not to mention her mother. Just picking up and going, with only a few hundred dollars and no real plan? To a place she'd never been and where she knew no one? So much uncertainty and risk! Yet where uncertainty and risk gave others pause, they only excited Dani. Besides, were there no jobs in Chapel Hill slinging greasy breakfasts? Were there not people she could love, and who would love her?

It was another of her epiphanies, spurred by a sign: What in the world was keeping her from leaving this place tomorrow?

The answer, of course, was nothing. Not a thing.

And like that, Dani made her decision. So now her second stop, at Bob's Drive-In at the Benton bridge to meet the girls (which was what they were, still—God love them, but they were still just girls) would not be a casual post-commencement gath-ering, but a good-bye. Maybe Ben would be there too, with some of the guys, pretending to just hang out, playing it cool and ca-sual but hoping to catch a glimpse of her and maybe, if he were lucky, talk to her some, even though he had to know it was over now, really over, with him having another year of high school left, and even if he hadn't had another year in this place it was over anyway, because as much as it saddened Dani to admit it to herself, let alone to Ben, she just didn't love him. Things really were that simple sometimes, despite all that people did and said to complicate matters.

She got into her car and drove back up the access road, spin-ning gravel under the tires, excited now about her decision to leave even though she didn't want to see Ben and have to tell him; it would be easier, she thought, if he just heard about it to-morrow or the next day from one of her girlfriends and had time to sort it out on his own. That kind of grieving was best done in private, Dani believed, away from friends and family, and especially from the person who caused the hurt. She knew Ben loved her, but she also knew what his love wanted to do to her—make her the wife of a millworker, with five kids and bad hair and nothing she could call her own except the blown-out veins in her legs. A small part of her hated Ben for that. And she knew that his suffering would be less and shorter-lived than her own would be if she gave in to his love, became what he wanted.

She reached the main road and continued east, toward Bob's Drive-In. Off to the left, just over the hills on the other side of the valley, she saw two black specks receding against the glowing blue—the loons, still together, still gliding up and away from here, gone almost completely now.

Dani smiled and thought about what she should bring with her, and what she should leave behind.

She would go straight home from Bob's and get to packing. It wouldn't take long. One suitcase, jeans and blouses, socks and bras and panties, a few short skirts for the hot Carolina summer. Her journal, a few magazines, the worn and much-loved copy of *A Tree Grows in Brooklyn*. Bathroom stuff, toothbrush and deodorant, hair ties, contact case and solution. Her mother would ask, *What are you doing?* And Dani would tell her: *I'm leaving, Mama. I'm a woman now, and today all the signs are pointing due south.* Simple as that. And her mother might be sad, and a little scared, her baby going away. But Dani thought she'd be equally happy and proud. *Get going, girl,* she might say after a moment's thought and a tearful hug. *Get out there and do all those things I never did.*

I'm already gone, Dani thought to herself in the car, under the sun, among the waving fields of corn and cattails and strawberries.

Benton was only a short drive from the pond, and soon Dani was turning through the last lazy bend leading up to what passed for Benton's downtown. As the road straightened out and the bridge came into view, she saw a row of maybe ten cars stopped at the foot of the bridge. On the other side of the river cars in the oncoming lane were backed up to Bob's Drive-In. And on the bridge itself, flanked by two state police cruisers, their blues flashing, was a single black sedan, parked squarely alongside the pedestrian walkway, its driver's-side door hanging open.

Dani pulled to a stop and got out to join the other onlookers, approaching the bridge with slow steps, eyeing a black-clad figure, presumably the owner of the black sedan, who stood on the narrow ledge on the wrong side of the railing. Two staties in their big hats stood behind him, their hands raised in cautious entreaty. They were speaking to the man's back. The toes of the man's black shoes hung out over the riverbed; only his heels were in contact with the ledge. His arms, in their black sleeves, were stretched out behind him. His hands grasped the top of the railing so tightly that Dani could see the knuckles straining against the skin, even at this distance.

And she moved closer, faster now, her feet carrying her past the others, who gawked and pointed and gradually stopped at what they perceived as a safe distance. Dani kept moving forward. And saw that the man on the wrong side of the railing was in fact a priest; he turned his head briefly toward the staties, and Dani could see the white flash of collar at his throat. She saw, also, that he was old. His hair was full but stark white, and the skin just above his collar was loose and grizzled, pinched into a cluster of pendulous wrinkles by the tight fabric of his faith.

And Dani kept walking, past the steel joints where the road met the bridge. Here the bravest of the onlookers had stopped, their hands to their mouths, as if some invisible barrier kept them from proceeding any further. She moved through this barrier and took one step onto the bridge, then another. She could hear the staties now, the fear in their voices. "Father, please," they said, their hands open and helpless. The priest paid them no attention, but gazed down at the river below, which in the summer heat had dried to a trickle, laying bare the hard cracked bed, the rocks glazed green with lichen, a few dead fish rotting in the sun.

On the other side of the bridge, at Bob's Drive-In, Dani saw her friends, girls and boys alike standing on the hoods of their cars, shading their eyes with cupped hands. One boy turned to another and said something. When he turned back, he was smiling.

They are children, Dani thought. *This is entertainment.*

The staties: one very tall, the other of average height, both projecting strength and control in their pressed uniforms and bulky black gun belts. But their eyes gave the lie to this illusion— they had no strength, and no control. They were afraid. They were only feet from the priest's back but did not move to touch him. "Father, please . . ."

Dani moved closer still, around the police cruiser, her legs carrying her forward of their own accord. She looked at the staties. *Do something,* she wanted to say, but she said nothing. She was afraid the sound of her voice might sever the delicate tendrils of reality which were, it seemed, the only thing that kept the old priest from plummeting off the side of the bridge. Because this, what was about to happen, couldn't be real. Could not. And so if she stayed silent, did not disturb the scene, maybe reality would reassert itself. *Do something, for Christ's sake.*

Dani stopped. The priest lifted his eyes from the riverbed. For the first time that day, the sun passed behind a cloud, a phantom cloud out of nowhere, and the Earth dimmed, and Dani glanced over to the hills and saw the sky was empty, and she looked back and saw, on the pavement near the tall statie's polished boots, something that would follow her to Carolina and beyond: laid out neatly, side by side, were the old priest's hat and wire-rimmed glasses.

For years, long after the world ended and remade itself, Dani would dream of reaching out to the priest, and wake with the starched feel of his black cotton shirtsleeve between her fingers.

Dani looked up, following the priest's gaze. She saw nothing but blue. When she looked back the priest was gone. For a long, long moment, everything was frozen just like that. And then the sun came out from behind the phantom cloud, and the Earth brightened, and things started moving again, but slowly.

Indian Summer

Howl, ye shepherds, and cry; and wallow yourselves in the ashes, ye principal of the flock: for the days of your slaughter and of your dispersions are accomplished; and ye shall fall like a pleasant vessel.

—Jeremiah 25:34

There were ten of us, eight if you didn't count the two in the middle of the living room holding pistols to each other's heads. Of the ten I figured I couldn't have been the only one who wondered if this was really happening. We'd been drinking, of course, and Rick's parents' house and its contents had taken on the strange incandescence which infuses everything after you've had most of a bottle of Yukon Jack. Plus this was after they'd announced officially that God was dead, but before the CAPA was formed, and things in general, drunk or not, were more than a little weird and unreal-seeming. It could have easily been a dream. I could have been in a coma, asleep under the tentacles of sighing machines while my mother sat at the bedside and held my cold hand in hers and my brain projected a movie onto the insides of my eyelids about how the world had cracked and I and my friends, bereaved and despairing, were about to commit mass suicide. So I'm sure I wasn't the only one thinking this might not be real, right up to the moment when Rick counted one, two, THREE, and on THREE Ben and Manny blew each other's brains out.

I even giggled a bit, just before the room exploded with blood and smoke. I mean, we were supposed to be heading back to college, except that there were no colleges to return to. It was all very difficult to wrap your head around.

For a minute after the rounds went off, I could barely see anything, the smoke was so thick. It smelled like the cap guns kids use to play cowboys and Indians, and under that the heavy stench of singed hair and skin. The smoke rose slowly to the ceiling, folding in on itself and shifting like low clouds, and Ben and Manny's corpses came into view on the floor. If I hadn't known who they were I wouldn't have recognized them.

We all stood there, beers in hand, smoke curling off us in little wisps. Everyone appeared shell-shocked, except for Rick, whose expression of grim calm emerged from the cloud rigid and unchanged. Chad, who'd been standing behind and to the right of Manny, looked like Jackson Pollock had used his Shipyard Brewing Company T-shirt to make a splatter painting. I'd taken Explorations in Contemporary Art the previous semester, and we'd spent a lot of time on abstract expressionism, so I could imagine the description in our textbook for this particular piece: Pollock, Jackson. *Suicide*. Brain on cotton, 2005.

There was so much blood. Blood on the walls, the bookshelves, the framed 8-by-10 of Rick and his folks, taken when we were still in high school. Blood running in languid red lines down the face of the high-definition TV, which had sat silent and useless since the power went out. Blood in little dots on Rick's mother's collection of ceramic figurines. And blood on the floor, pooled an inch deep, already coagulating at the edges like pudding left uncovered.

Rick waded into the mess and picked up the pistols. "Get a mop," he told me.

.

We'd all lost something, of course. My mother was gone, dead in her sleep after the refills for her insulin pump stopped arriving in the mail. Manny's father had a stroke around the time the real trouble began, and no ambulances were running by then, so he died kicking on the bathroom floor of their split-level ranch; after that Manny's mom left with his younger sister for Florida, where she'd heard things weren't so bad. Chad, Allen, and Ben all lost their families to the car accidents which became common after traffic signals went down and the roads began to pile up with wrecks. Wesley's father and stepmother had flown to Tucson on a golfing trip and never come back. Leo's parents were killed in an explosion at the Shell station while foraging for canned soup and Twinkies. The fire burned for a week, spreading through the middle-class residences of Cherry Hill and killing Cole's family and Jack's mother and twin sisters. And Rick had seen his parents shot to death by a neighbor intent on siphoning the gasoline from their Audi. Rick killed the man, an economics professor who used to come by for vodka martinis on Sunday afternoons during football season, with a garden rake to the back of the head.

One by one, following our personal tragedies, we ended up at Rick's house. Manny and I moved in while Rick's parents were still alive; we were in the garage, looking for something to cover a broken window on the second floor, when the neighbor killed them over a quarter tank of premium unleaded.

I often wonder how things might have turned out if we'd been in the driveway and seen the guy coming. If maybe Manny had clipped him in the knees like the star outside linebacker he'd been. If I'd busted his shooting hand with the official Reggie Jackson Louisville Slugger leaning against the workbench in the garage. Because then Rick's parents would have lived, and we wouldn't have been left by ourselves to decide what next. We were just boys, after all.

The next morning Leo and Cole showed up together, followed by Jack that afternoon, and we all helped dig two holes in the backyard next to Rick's father's tomato plants. You don't know the meaning of the term *awkward silence* until you're standing over twin piles of freshly turned dirt with nothing to say. I nearly suggested we offer a prayer, then gave myself a mental kick in the ass for being so stupid. It didn't matter anyway, because Rick had already gone back in the house.

We dragged the neighbor's body into the road and left it there.

In many ways, the next few weeks resembled the lives we'd led before. We drank too much, played music and video games, stayed up all night and slept all day. Wesley and I took a truck from the abandoned U-Haul and spent a weekend emptying out Haskell Liquors and transferring the stock to Rick's garage.

Indian summer hit. We threw horseshoes and lazed in patio chairs, trying to drink enough to convince ourselves this was just an extended summer break.

The new reality kept interfering, however. Although the hot weather brought with it high, cloudless skies, a gray haze hung from fires that burned unchecked all over the valley, powdering our skin with soot. One by one the radio and TV stations blinked out of existence. Our stores of food and booze dwindled. Often the night sky flashed a literal electric blue as transformers exploded on telephone poles, and soon the power went out at Rick's house. We lit candles, listened to the crickets exult in summer's last gasp, and grew solemn over warm beers.

None more so than Rick. Normally cheerful and fearless (in high school he'd been designated beer buyer, and the only one besides Cole to ever dive from the dreaded sixty-foot cliff at the reservoir in Halowell), since burying his parents he'd stalked through the house, stiff and slow and silent. He drank until his legs gave way and slept wherever he fell—beside the bathtub, on the concrete of the garage floor. He developed an obsession with cleaning, yet seemed afraid to disturb any object in the house; one morning I watched from the hallway as he lifted his father's can of shaving gel to wipe the backsplash on the bathroom sink, then spent ten minutes replacing the can, moving it to the left an inch, then to the right, rotating it slightly, stepping back to examine the scene from several angles, then adjusting some more.

He went for days without speaking to anyone. Leo, who since we were kids had believed that others could be unhappy only through some fault of his, asked me what he'd done.

"It's not you, Leo," I said. "Rick's just sad. Everyone's sad, you know?"

But that wasn't all of it. Beyond mere sadness, we were starting to feel trapped in a perpetual *now* (as our past receded and any sort of meaningful future became a logical impossibility), a sort of purgatory where you drank and tanned and played Tetris with the same ten guys until the end of time. The walls were closing in, the SpaghettiOs were getting old, and soon Rick wasn't the only one tottering around like a mute, zombified version of himself.

Then the power went out.

A few days later we woke hungover and thirsty to find the sinks had gone dry. This was the last straw for Rick. He called us into the living room, popped open a Pabst tall boy, took a long swallow, and gazed around.

"I've got a proposition," he said.

We listened. It didn't seem too crazy, all things considered, and the more we drank, the better it sounded. We chewed it over for hours, until daylight faded. No one bothered to light the hurricane lamp that sat on the piano bench.

"We're not doing it unless everyone agrees," Rick said. "All of us together, just like always."

We sat quietly, alone with our thoughts, for a while after that. I thought about my mother. I thought about my plans to become an architectural engineer (not a dream, strictly speaking, but an aspiration, one that had been fairly important to me). I thought about all the horrifying Mad Max–type scenarios that awaited us when we eventually ran out of food.

Then Rick called each of our names, and one by one we said yes. It was easy in the dark, somehow, shockingly easy, as if we were deciding nothing more weighty than which toppings to get on a pizza. We lit the lamp, sealed our agreement with a dull clink of near-empty beer cans, and went to bed.

It seemed like the best of a host of bad prospects.

■

Now, though, as I mopped up the remains of two guys I'd met playing kickball in grade school, I wasn't so sure anymore. I'd changed the water in the bucket three times yet succeeded only in diluting the mess and spreading it around; the pine boards were streaked with a soapy pink mixture, as if someone had spilled a gallon of strawberry smoothie. Two darker smears extended to the mudroom, where the bodies had been dragged outside. It would have taken hours to clean up properly, and there were still eight of us to go.

I pushed the mop around a little longer, miming an honest effort to clean the floor, while the others leaned against door frames and unsoiled patches of wall, smoking, watching. Finally Rick held a Pabst out to me. "Good enough," he said. "Pretty soon no one will care anyway."

His other hand was fisted around a cluster of eight red drinking straws, cut to various lengths. "Gather round," he said, and we did, slowly. For the first time I noticed how bad we all smelled. It'd been a week since anyone had showered, and the only stick of deodorant in the house, having belonged to Rick's father, was off-limits.

Leo and Cole drew the short straws. Rick had tucked the pistols into his waistband, and he removed them now. Cole, with a sigh equal parts resignation and relief, took one. He tested the weight of the gun and eyeballed Leo.

Leo looked at Cole, then turned and ran, through the mudroom and out into the night, screaming a shrill apology about how he was just as sad and scared as the rest of us but didn't have the guts for this no matter how much he drank.

"Wait here," Rick said. He went after Leo, still holding the pistol.

I was first onto the porch, in time to see Rick's figure receding in the dark at the end of the street. He turned left and disappeared, going like an Olympic sprinter, his bare feet slapping the blacktop. We waited and listened but couldn't hear anything over the riot of bullfrogs in the tiny man-made pond two houses down.

Fifteen minutes passed, then half an hour. Wesley went into

the garage to grab fresh beers for everyone, and came back bleeding from a gash on his palm.

"Tripped over the snowblower," he said with a rueful grin. He handed out blood-streaked beers.

"That's pretty nasty," Allen said. "You ought to clean that up. Wrap it in a towel or something."

Wesley looked at him. "What the hell for?" he asked.

Cole, seated in a rattan chair between me and Wesley, drank his beer in three pulls and let loose a roaring belch.

"Well, fuck this," he said. He eased the pistol past his teeth, drew several quick breaths around the barrel, and fired. The bullet ripped a softball-sized hole in the back of his skull and shattered the window behind him. Jagged triangles of glass clung to the window frame, dripping with blood and brain.

"Jesus Christ," Allen said. His beer, dropped from numb fingers, sat in a puddle of foam on the top step. No one else spoke. Their faces registered only a mild, fleeting surprise, then went blank again as we waited some more for Rick to come back.

"You think he caught him?" Chad asked.

"Probably," Jack said. "Leo isn't exactly a star athlete."

"If he caught him, we would have heard something," Wesley said. "A gunshot. A scream. Something."

I took a sip of beer to steel myself. "This could maybe be a mistake, guys," I said. "I realize we're probably past the time for debate. But still."

Wesley looked at me. "You wouldn't be saying that if Rick were here."

"Fucking right I wouldn't," I said. "Because Rick's lost his mind. He's out there hunting Leo. Leo, our friend. The guy who took us all to his dad's time-share in Florida for graduation. And if Rick catches him, he'll shoot him down like a dog."

"We're still friends," Jack said. "That's why we're doing this. It's kind of a sacred thing."

"Leo agreed, just like the rest of us," Wesley said. "Look, I feel bad for the dude. But he voted yes. Ben and Manny went through with it, and Cole anted up. No one can back out now."

I eyed the pistol on the floor next to Cole's chair. Wesley, noticing my gaze, picked up the gun and rested it in his lap.

"I just want to see my folks again," Allen said. "It's kind of embarrassing to say it, but I don't care much. I miss my parents."

I didn't have the heart or the energy to point out to him how unlikely it seemed, all things considered, that there was an afterlife of any kind.

Wesley turned over his hand in the moonlight, gingerly fingering the cut on his palm, which had stopped bleeding. "If you could have any food right now," he said to no one in particular, "what would it be?"

Everybody but me chimed in—here was a topic they could drum up some enthusiasm for. Chad wanted a pupu platter, minus the egg rolls, substitute extra beef teriyaki. Jack had been dreaming about the Coca-Cola brisket sandwich they used to serve on Wednesdays at the Bodega Bar. Allen missed his mother's lasagna, thick with ricotta and onion and three kinds of meat, topped with shingled slices of provolone that crisped at the edges as the dish slow-cooked for most of the day.

"Oh shit, her lasagna was awesome," Chad said. "Can I change my answer?"

Run, Leo, I thought. *Run like the wind, buddy.*

■

Just after midnight a perfect circle, clear like glass and vaguely rainbow-hued at its edge, formed around the moon. An autumn chill settled into the valley, silencing the frogs and chasing us inside. We left Cole where he sat and lit fresh candles to replace the ones that had burned down.

"Leo's gone," Rick said when he returned fifteen minutes later. He placed an unopened Pabst on the coffee table and leaned over with his hands on his knees, still trying to catch his breath. The sides of his feet were scuffed black, punctuated with spots of startling pink where blisters had formed and torn open.

"Meaning what?" Wesley asked.

"Meaning he got away," Rick said. "I went clear across town to the industrial park. Must have run ten miles. He's gone."

"Fucking coward," Wesley said. Chad grumbled in agreement.

"Doesn't matter," Rick said. He stood up straight and kneaded a stitch in his ribs. "I'm going to drink a beer real quick. Then we'll draw straws again and get this done."

"I think maybe we should forget the straws and just decide who's next," Wesley said, looking pointedly at me. "Before anyone else gets cold feet."

Rick popped open his beer and took a long swallow. "Having second thoughts?" he asked me.

I watched him for a moment, then figured what the hell; either way I'd most likely end up dead. "Yeah," I said. "I am."

"Want to talk it over?"

"Will it make a difference?"

He sighed. "Probably not. But let's do it anyway. Outside."

I followed Rick through the mudroom and onto the porch, trying to ignore the rhythmic clink of the gun butt against his retro-hip Heavy Equipment Operator belt buckle. He pointed to Cole's body, which sat cold and smelling faintly of shit in the moonlight.

"He do that himself?" Rick asked.

"Yes."

"Good old Cole. Cast-iron balls to the end."

"I don't know," I said. "I think he was just miserable and scared, like the rest of us."

"And bored," Rick said.

"That too."

We were quiet for a minute. Then Rick said, "We both know I'm nuts, right? We're in agreement on that?"

I glanced again at the gun in his waistband and said, "Is this a trick question?"

"No."

"Okay. Then, yeah. No offense, you're still my friend, and I love you. But you're batshit crazy, man."

Rick smiled sadly. "Right," he said. "But what you don't know is I went nuts a long time before all this shit started. First semester last fall, to be exact. Was the first time I realized I wanted to kill someone."

I said nothing.

"It went like this. A couple of guys at school asked me to go camping with them one weekend. I'd just started organic chemistry and had a ton of reading to do, so I sat in my room debating whether or not to go. Drinking a Heineken Dark. I remember it so vividly. Sunlight coming in through the blinds, the smell of pot and incense from the guys across the hall. So there I am, weighing three hundred pages of reading against this camping trip, and out of nowhere I think how easy it would be to kill those guys, up in the mountains with no one around. I'm looking at this class syllabus, right, but what I'm seeing is these two guys lying under the trees with their throats slashed. For no reason at all. I liked them. We chummed around campus, worked out together, drank together. Do you understand what I'm saying?"

I nodded.

"After that, I gotta tell you, showing up for class on time and studying hard and waiting tables to keep myself in beer money didn't seem so important anymore. I wasn't that person, to say the least. An instant transformation. And it got worse. I'd bring a girl back to my room and imagine strangling her even as I rubbed her shoulders and kissed the back of her neck. Do you have any idea how terrifying and—really, it sounds funny—*depressing* it is when all you want is to be a normal nineteen-year-old guy and have sex with some semi-anonymous but very pretty and sweet girl, to smell her and taste the sweat on her lips, but even as you're doing it, even as you're going carefully through every motion, all you can think about is killing her?"

I nodded. I'd done the very thing he described—brought girls home with me from a party, made love, and woke up in the morning with the sun on my face, feeling happy and spent and bloated with possibility. It was a wonderful thing, and I could imagine how terrible it must have felt to be excluded from it.

"So that's what I did for the next year," Rick said. "Went through the motions—school, work, friends, girls, feeling scared and sick and murderous, barely under control. It's like an open circuit, just keeps coming and coming no matter what you do to try and turn it off. I thought about how when you act normal and look normal people just give themselves up to you. I thought about how the law is only after the fact. So that by the time they told us God was dead and all hell broke loose, it seemed like kind of a blessing to me. Because I had this horrible awareness now. I understood those guys who climb clock towers or walk into a McDonald's with guns blazing. I felt more like them than the people who stand around after the rampages, crying and asking why, why, why. Because I understood there is no why. There's the impulse, and the act. But nothing else."

And in that moment, listening to him, I felt within me a shift as sudden and irrevocable as the one Rick described. I was, in the parlance of my generation, over it. Utterly fucking so. I wanted to be shut of this stupid caricature of a life, in which my mother was dead, my hopes razed, and my best friend a melancholy lunatic who had no idea why he'd become such a monster.

"It feels really good to finally admit this to someone," Rick said. "Well, not just *someone*. I mean, God, I'm glad it's you, man."

"God," I said. "Ha."

Rick leaned in and examined my face. "Are you crying?" he asked.

"Never mind," I said. "Let's get on with it."

∎

Wesley insisted on being part of the next pair, so we drew straws for the other half and Chad came up shortest. The two of them faced off in the living room, and on the count of THREE pulled their respective triggers without hesitation. By now a mood of grim impatience had set in, and we removed the bodies from the living room even before the smoke dissipated. We didn't bother going all the way outside, just dragged Wesley and Chad by their ankles into the mudroom and left them to bleed out on the slate tile like freshly slaughtered hogs.

In all the falling and flailing that had occurred in the moments after they shot each other, one of them had knocked over the coffee table, and the straws rested, barely visible, in a pool of blood the exact color and consistency of molasses. Since there were only four of us left anyhow, Rick said what the hell and told Allen and Jack he'd made an executive decision, and they were next. No argument from them. Without any further prodding they stepped to the center of the room, lifted the pistols from the floor, and waited for a count.

One . . . two . . . THREE.

Another roaring flash. Something warm and wet hit my face hard, like raindrops driven on a gust of wind. I'd stepped too close to Allen, and my ears were ringing like Notre Dame, so I barely heard Rick mutter "Son of a bitch" in disbelief as Leo and a cop, standing together in the entryway, came into view through the smoke.

The cop had his service revolver drawn and pointed in our direction. Beneath a week's growth of beard his face was nearly as round and smooth as ours, and his eyes, taking in the scene, flashed with fear and uncertainty. His uniform was rumpled, the blue shirt untucked and stained darkly under the arms, the badge conspicuously missing. From across the room I could see his hands tremble as he struggled to summon the command presence they'd taught him at the academy.

"What have you boys done?" he asked.

Rick smiled. "How old are you, twenty-three, twenty-four? And you're calling *us* boys?" He reached for the pistol Jack had used, on the floor near his feet.

"Don't do that," the cop said. He pointed his revolver directly at Rick. "Hey. Don't."

Rick called his bluff, hoisting the pistol and holding it steady at arm's length. The cop swallowed hard.

"Rick," Leo said. "C'mon, man."

"Leo, what are you thinking?" Rick said. "Hello? Hey, you changed your mind? Fine. Don't want to die after all? Definitely understandable. Not very cool, you know, everyone else stuck to the bargain, but understandable. And then you go and pull this shit."

Leo drew a ragged breath and broke down in the sort of uncontrolled weeping that embarrasses everyone within earshot. "I'm sorry," he said.

"Jesus," Rick said. "Get yourself together, man."

The cop adjusted his grip on the revolver. "Drop it," he told Rick.

"I don't want to be alone," Leo sobbed. "That's all."

"Well, you know, I was pretty impressed when you took off like that," Rick said. "I mean, for the first time I can remember, you grew some balls and made a decision for yourself, Leo. Except you fucked it all up by coming back."

"Last warning," the cop said, not all that convincingly. He licked his lips. "Put the gun down."

Rick turned his attention back to the cop. "You I don't really understand," he said. "Why are you wearing that uniform? It's not like there's much left to serve or protect, bud."

"I've still got a job to do," the cop said. "And don't call me bud. Maybe I am only a few years older than you, but I'm still your elder, and on top of that an officer of the law. So I'd appreciate it if you'd show the proper respect and address me as *Sir* or *Officer Bates*. Also, if you'd put the weapon down."

"Fucking Boy Scout," Rick said. "So anyway, here's the deal. One way or another I'm going to die tonight. It doesn't really matter if you shoot me, or if my buddy here does it."

"I'm not playing your game," the cop said.

"Hate to be the one to break the news, Officer Bates, but you already are," Rick said. "The rules are pretty simple. I give a three count. On three, we shoot each other. Got it?"

The cop wiped one hand on his pants and said nothing.

Leo looked at me. "Please," he said.

I shrugged.

Rick had only reached TWO when the cop shot him in the shoulder. The bullet spun Rick a quarter turn to the left, but he stayed on his feet and took aim again. The cop had time to fire a panicked second shot, missing high, before his throat exploded in a mess of blood and cartilage and he went down gurgling like a clogged pool filter.

Leo leapt away from the cop's thrashing and pressed himself into the corner.

"Rick," he said. "Are you all right?"

"Leo," Rick said, wincing as he examined the wound in his shoulder, "you really ought to go now."

"I'm sorry," Leo said. "Listen, I'm really sorry, I just—"

Rick pointed the pistol straight up and squeezed off two rounds. By the time the report from the second shot faded, Leo was gone into the night for good.

Rick sank to the floor and leaned against the arm of the sofa. His hair was speckled with chips of yellowish ceiling plaster. A few feet away the cop kicked weakly, expelled a last, wet, whistling breath through the hole in his throat, and was still.

I plunked myself down on the sofa and let my head loll, staring at the twin holes in the ceiling. "Why'd you let him go?" I asked.

Rick turned his head to the side and spit on the floor. "That's the funny thing," he said. "I never want to kill when I'm angry. It's strange. You'd think that would be the time I'd feel most like offing somebody."

"You'd think," I said.

"Fuck," Rick said. "This hurts."

■

By now you're thinking I must not have gone through with it. Here I am, telling you this story, using the past tense, so it follows that I must have slipped quietly away after Rick got woozy from blood loss, or else just finished him off myself and gone out to join Leo. I must have changed my mind, flaked, chickened out.

But that's not the case. I went through with it. I honored the agreement we'd made.

So how is it, then, that I'm still here, a man approaching late middle age in a world restored by the CAPA to a reasonable facsimile of its former self? A man with a nine-to-whenever in a design firm he co-founded, with a wife and a teenage daughter, a late-model Saab, and a three handicap? A man who sees less and less of the boy he once was when he contemplates his face in the bathroom mirror?

It's easy to understand when one considers that the pistols we used that night, a twin set of Desert Eagle XIX .50 calibers belonging to Rick's father, held clips of seven rounds each. And that one of the guns had been fired four more times than the other—once by Cole, and three times by Rick when he killed the cop and frightened off Leo. So that when Rick and I sat side by side on the floor in our friends' blood and he put a hand on the back of my neck and pressed our foreheads together and called me by a childhood nickname I'd nearly forgotten, one of the guns was empty, and the other, the one in my trembling hand, still held four rounds.

False Idols

Thou shalt have no other gods before me.

   —Exodus 20:3

Mrs. DerSimonian sits across from me, wringing her hands so roughly that they've mounted a protest in the form of alternating red and white splotches. Mothers generally have a tougher time than fathers, but Mrs. DerSimonian has a worse time of it than most. This is due in part to her nervous disposition, and in part to the mothering philosophy of Armenian-Americans, which encourages doting and fussing. She sweats. Her hands flutter in her lap. She applies great gleaming swaths of lip balm, over and over, until the whole office smells like strawberries.

Today's exercise is Delusion Jettison. Pretty rudimentary stuff, it's true, but in the two years I've been seeing Mrs. DerSimonian the ratio of progression to setback has been poor. Mostly, I came to realize, because of inadequate reinforcement of lessons learned. So we go back over the easy stuff a lot.

"Mrs. DerSimonian," I say. "Come on, now. Tell me how wonderful your son is."

She won't meet my gaze. Like spooked squirrels her eyes dart to her boy, Levon. He sits in the cage by the window, warmed by the afternoon sun, content with a coloring book and a box of Crayolas.

"Levon is fine," I tell her, my voice gentle but firm. "Granted, he's making a mess of that rabbit, giving it pastel green fur and coloring all outside the lines. But he's fine. Now tell me, what's so special about him?"

Her eyes come back in my direction but focus on the wall behind me. "You're just going to shoot me down," she says. "Tell me how wrong I am."

"That's the process," I say. "It's for your benefit, Mrs. DerSimonian. For everyone's benefit, especially Levon's. You know that."

She draws a deep, shuddering breath, closes her eyes, and puts a hand to her mouth. "I don't know if I can, today," she says through her fingers. "We had a scare earlier, and I'm still quite upset."

"Tell me about it," I say.

She opens her eyes again. Her gaze falls on the sign hanging on the wall behind me, which bears, in embroidered calligraphic letters, the motto of the Child Adulation Prevention Agency: *Children Are Like Any Other Group of People—A Couple of Winners, a Whole Lot of Losers.*

"I stopped at the store to buy a coffee," she says. "I skipped breakfast because I didn't get up until quarter to eight and Levon has his swim class at eight-thirty on Monday mornings."

"Now right there," I say. "A swim class for three-year-olds? Three-year-olds don't need classes of any kind. He should be in the backyard, splashing around in a mud puddle."

Now she looks directly at me. By her expression you'd think I suggested she give Levon a chain saw to play with.

"Do you realize how dangerous standing water is?" she asks. "Absolutely *teeming* with pathogens. Just last week, a boy died in Florida after swimming around in floodwaters. Leptospirosis."

Like a lot of parents these days, Mrs. DerSimonian makes it her business to know all the things that could kill her son, by name and in detail.

But I wave this away. "Go on with what you were saying. This morning. Coffee."

"Oh, God." The hand flies to her mouth again. "I'm getting all shaky thinking about it."

She falls silent once more. I wait. She looks at me, looks away, and continues.

"So I got out of the car and left it running with the air-conditioning on for Levon. Normally I would never, *ever* leave him in the car by himself, but I was only going inside for thirty seconds, and it just didn't seem worth it to open the hatch on his fireproof pod and undo all the straps on his car seat and take off his crash helmet. Especially the helmet. He hates it so much he goes into these screaming fits whenever he sees me coming at him with it. So I locked the car and left it running and went in for my coffee. But when I came out I realized I'd left my spare key at home.

"I started crying," she says, and now her eyes blossom with fresh tears. "I called the operator to have her send a signal to the car to unlock the doors, but I was crying too hard and she couldn't understand me, and meanwhile there's Levon, trapped inside, so close and yet I couldn't touch him or hold him, and he saw how upset I was and *he* started crying. Eventually the operator got the gist of what I was saying and unlocked the doors, but by then she'd called the police and fire department and they all showed up, two cops, an ambulance, and a fire engine, and there I was feeling terrible, just terrible, for putting my son in danger and bothering these good people, all for a coffee I never drank because I dropped it on the sidewalk in a panic."

I take a tissue from the box on my desk and hand it to Mrs. DerSimonian.

"I still feel terrible," she sniffles, dabbing at her eyes.

I consider pointing out to her that Levon was in no danger at all, that emergency services are there for the sole purpose of being bothered by people in distress, that leaving her son alone for thirty seconds is hardly an unpardonable crime.

Instead I say, "Mrs. DerSimonian. Tell me how wonderful your son is."

She makes a strangled, frustrated sound in her throat, drops the tissue to her lap, and says, "He's very, very bright. Okay?"

"Wrong!" I say, slamming my fist on the desktop. "He scored a 92 on his latest Wechsler Preschool and Primary Scale of Intelligence test, which places him firmly in the median range among American children. In seven previous tests, he's never scored higher than a 98. Like most of us, Levon will have to rely on the gifted few to drive human intellectual progress in his lifetime. He will be a passenger, not a participant."

Mrs. DerSimonian gives me an evil look. "How about you," she says, "go fuck yourself."

I sit back and straighten my hair. "I'm just trying to help," I say.

■

As the Child Adulation Prevention Psychiatrist for Watertown and surrounding communities, I am both the most vital and most hated man in Kennebec County. Vital, because without me my zone of responsibility would soon descend back into the child-worshipping anarchy from which I rescued it only two years ago. Hated, because I force people to see their children for what they really are: flawed, mortal, and essentially useless creatures.

Before becoming the regional CAPP I ran a small private practice. I had a wife, a baby on the way, and a med school debt of insurmountable proportions. Things were good. Optimism ruled the day. I helped people in a manner that made them happy and grateful. They came to me with phobias and sexual dysfunctions and suicidal ideations, and I cared for them. *Cared* is the word. This was not a job. It was my life. I took on patients with no insurance, worked sixteen-hour days, paid out-of-pocket to install and maintain a crisis line in my home, so people could always call if they needed to. My wife Laura, glowingly pregnant, loved me. She believed in what I did. We were ready to start a family.

But these were hard times, the tail end of a decade of economic depression and its attendant social ills: mammoth unemployment, rising rates of drug abuse, domestic violence, and property crime, race and labor riots, and in the now-famous takeover of the Cleveland VA Medical Center by angry Gulf War veterans, organized and violent insurrection.

Then the world learned God had been found dead in Sudan. As far as anyone could determine, he'd taken mortal form to observe firsthand the armed conflict between Sudan's Islamic government and the Christian Nuer tribe in the south. Fleeing to Kenya with Nuer refugees, he'd gotten snagged in a razor-wire fence bordering a minefield. Others in his group tried to free him, but were forced to leave him behind when bombs from government attack planes rained down. He died, stripped naked by thieves and scorched by the equatorial sun, near the border town of Kapoeta.

One small death among thousands, his passing would have gone unnoticed if the feral dogs who fed on his corpse hadn't suddenly begun speaking a mishmash of Greek and Hebrew, and walking along the surface of the White Nile as if it were made of glass.

Naturally, the news of God's death hit the world like a sledge-hammer. An initial wave of panic, civil unrest, and general bad behavior swept the globe. Martial law was declared, and the National Guard took up residence in every American city. Suicide among nuns and clergy reached epidemic proportions, as did the looting of stores for comfort foods such as Little Debbie snack cakes. Most, myself included, believed the end was nigh, and for a while we hid in our homes, hunched over and wincing, convinced that at any moment we would explode, or simply blip out of existence.

And then a strange thing happened: nothing. Gradually we came to realize that the sun still rose in the morning and set at night, the tide still came in and went out on schedule, and we and everyone we knew (for the most part) were still alive and breathing. Talking heads and self-declared experts offered any number of theories, but the gist of it, intuited by most people, was this: God had created the universe and set it spinning, but it would continue chugging along despite the fact that he was no longer around to keep things tidy.

People emerged from their hiding places and got back to their lives. The National Guard stood down. Laura and I breathed a sigh of relief and resumed planning for the baby's arrival, compiling lists of names, pricing nursery wallpaper, buying mobiles and jumpers. For a while the only noticeable change was the absolute lack of anything to do on Sundays.

Then the real trouble began. I saw it in my patients: a spiritual void left in the wake of God's demise. People everywhere were casting about for something to place their recently orphaned faith in. Agnostics joined the atheists and put their money on science, but they were, as always, hopelessly outnumbered. Many people, including most of the population of Africa, built temples dedicated to the dogs who had feasted on God's flesh, churches where the hymnals consisted entirely of barks and whines transcribed phonetically onto the page. And here, out of the swamps of Louisiana's Atchafalaya basin and into this burgeoning chaos came a sort of secular evangelist known as The Child. The Child was just that—a boy of three or so, serene and flawless, with cocoa skin and a vocabulary so rich it seemed he must have swallowed an Oxford English Dictionary. His message, delivered first in town halls and opera houses, and later, as his popularity grew, in arenas and baseball stadiums, was simple: *God has abandoned us. The way to salvation is through the child.*

By which he meant, of course, every child.

And America, already teetering on the verge of child worship, was only too eager to hear him. Soon a phenomenon unprecedented in the history of psychiatry arose: Adults, buffeted by socioeconomic insecurities, with the nuclear canopy still overhead and no God to protect them from it, turned to their children for comfort and guidance.

As a psychiatrist, I began to see examples of this strange behavior well before it started to make headlines. Ricky Mascis, an out-of-work single father who I treated free of charge, was troubling over which bills to pay, as he didn't have enough to cover all of them.

"So it's really just, you know, you gotta prioritize," he told me. "Which isn't too hard at first. Obviously, if it's between buying a new TV or paying the power bill, you pay the bill. No brainer. But now I've got to decide things like, should I buy food this week, or should I put that hundred dollars into fixing the car so I can get out and look for a job?"

"It's a tough choice," I agreed. "What do you think?"

"I don't know. I asked Boo where he thought I should put the money." Boo was Ricky's four-year-old son, Ricky Jr. "He said I should buy ten sets of Hungry Hungry Hippos."

"Cute," I said. "That's the luxury of being a child, of course. You don't have to make hard decisions."

"I don't know, Doc," Ricky said. "Boo's a really smart kid. I mean, supersmart, and I've had it with worrying about all this crap. I'm thinkin' the hippos might be the way to go."

It got worse in a hurry. God, hamstrung by a spotty track record, and dead besides, was out; kids, tangible, blameless, and cute as all hell, were in. Soon the phenomenon blossomed into a two-tiered crisis. In the majority of adults, who comprised the less acute tier, the behavior was not all that dissimilar to the ways in which parents had indulged children before God died. Tantrums were permitted, even smiled at. Landfills bulged with excised bread crusts and untouched vegetable portions. Toys "R" Us shares rose 90 percent in three weeks. The worst upshot of this was a moderate loss in productivity, as time normally spent in the cubicle and behind the checkout counter was instead squandered at Chuck E. Cheese's or the local petting zoo. This problem would have been manageable without radical intervention, though, if it hadn't been for the smaller but more acute tier.

These parents were found in the country's traditional bastions of religious piety—the Deep South, the rural Northeast, Utah. In these places the transition to child worship was brisk and absolute, and Laura and I witnessed it firsthand. Seventy percent of the adult population stopped going to work, choosing instead to watch the same animated feature for weeks on end, play Game Boy, and partake of grilled cheese sandwiches, peanut butter and jelly, and chocolate chip cookies. Basic infrastructure dissolved. People were dying in the streets because there were no paramedics to take them to the hospital, and no doctors there when they arrived.

The National Guard was mobilized yet again, but when they arrived they found there wasn't much to be done, other than keeping people from entering or leaving the affected areas. The functions for which they were trained and equipped—policing duties, riot control—were not indicated, and it wasn't as if they could force people at gunpoint to stop spending time with their children. Another, more sublime solution needed to be found.

Soon word came through that FEMA, in conjunction with an unnamed intelligence agency, was convening an emergency meeting of mental health professionals in Washington. I had to go, if our baby was to have a future. I dusted off my hiking boots and filled a backpack with canned soup and turkey jerky from the abandoned 7-Eleven. Laura and I shared a cry.

"You're doing the right thing," she said.

I held her close, pressing her belly to me. "I'd curse God for forcing me to make such a choice," I said. "But, you know."

"Go," she said, and gently pushed me away. She laced her fingers together over the globe of her abdomen and smiled. "We'll be waiting."

She spoke the truth. When I returned from D.C. three months later, accompanied by an Army recon platoon and armed with a Ryder truck of antipsychotic medication and the government's brutal but effective therapy plan, I found Laura and the son she'd died giving birth to, curled together on the kitchen floor, waiting for me to bury them.

■

Mrs. DerSimonian is the last patient of the day, so when she's gone I make a few idle notes in her file, lock up the office, and head outside. I find Jeff Pauquette sitting on the trunk of my Celica. The sleeves of his signature flannel work shirt are rolled up, revealing hairy, muscular forearms. He's glowering at me from under the bill of a Teague Tractor Supply baseball cap.

"Looks like they did a real number on her this time, them," he calls to me across the parking lot.

This is a little game we play. Every day, while I'm in the office, Jeff vandalizes my car. Then he pretends someone else did it, and I pretend I don't know it was him. The damage is usually worse on Wednesdays, after our mandatory weekly appointment, but today he's really outdone himself. The right rear tire is gutted, slashed all the way around the rim. Jeff's also gone to the trouble of uprooting a traffic sign and breaking the driver's-side window with it. The sign juts from the window as I approach, instructing me to STOP.

I set my briefcase on the pavement and pull the sign out. "They must have been particularly angry today," I say to Jeff.

"Must have been, them," he agrees.

"I wonder why," I say. "I wonder what I did today to make them so angry. Would you mind? I need to get the spare out of the trunk."

Jeff takes his time getting up. "I might have some theories about that," he says. "I might be able to shed a little light for you, me. 'Cept I spent all day thinking about what crappy kids my two boys are, like you told me."

I remove the jack, tire iron, and spare from the trunk. "They're not crappy kids, Jeff. Just normal. Average."

This is not strictly true. His younger son Abe has a fastball he could probably ride to the pros. Abe is also preternaturally compassionate. He cries at television commercials and displays none of the ruthless tendencies toward frogs and bugs usually seen in adolescent boys. But he has a harelip, so I focus on that during sessions with his father.

Jeff watches me work. "You know," he says after a while, "this problem with your car is getting epidemic. You ought to call the police about it, you."

I tighten the last lug nut on the spare and look up at him. "We both know the police won't do anything about it, Jeff. They hate me as much as everyone else. They hate me as much as you do."

For the first time, Jeff smiles. "No," he says. "Nobody around here hates you as much as I do, me."

"Don't know about that," I say. "I had Reggie Boucher jailed last week for missing two consecutive sessions. He's probably got you beat in the hating me department." I put the stuff back in the trunk and slam the lid shut. "Is there anything else, Jeff? Anything you want to talk about?"

"No, that'll be all," he says. "I gotta get back home, me. Gotta feed those ungrateful parasite sons."

"Good night, then," I say. But I know he won't leave just yet, and he doesn't. He gets into his truck and waits while I brush the broken glass from inside my car and start it up. Then he follows me all the way home, tailgating and blaring his horn. When I reach my driveway and pull in through the gate, he jams the accelerator, speeding past with a roar.

I park in the circular driveway and walk into the garage. With a ten-foot wall surrounding the place, no one could get in, not even Jeff, but still I lift the dustcover from the Jaguar and inspect it for the smallest hints of malice. Finding none, I take a new tire from the stack against the back wall and bring it out to the Celica, placing it in the trunk with the other three.

Then I go inside, punch the code into the security keypad, triple-lock the door, and run to the basement before the motion sensors reset themselves.

Selia's on the couch in the rumpus room, watching people on television eat cow eyeballs for money. There are five people in town with no relationship whatsoever to any children. Fortunately for me, Selia's one of them.

"Hey," she says. "What's the damage today?"

"One tire, gutted," I say. "Driver's-side window, smashed."

"Ouch."

"Jeff's getting more ruthless every day."

"The man is without ruth," Selia says. "Completely sans ruth."

"How's your mom?"

"The same. Today she thought I was a burglar when I came out of the bathroom. And she's still calling me Betty."

"Any mail?" I ask.

"Just the usual. Coupons. A dozen hate letters."

I kick off my shoes and sidle next to her. "You sure you still want to be the girlfriend of the most loathed man in town?"

"It's not so bad, other than the sneaking around," she says. "Let's do this, buckaroo. I have to get back before she starts mixing herself toilet-water martinis again."

We take each other's clothes off. Selia puts in her diaphragm and a triple dose of spermicidal foam. I double up on the condoms. We dim the lights. It's nice.

Afterward she kisses my forehead, then my hand, and asks if I need her to get some dinner. When Selia's not around I have to drive sixty miles to the Shop 'n Save just across the county line in Dover, because no one here will sell me food. But tonight there's half a bag of spanakopita in the freezer, along with some Tater Tots. I tell her I'm fine.

"You'd better hit the servants' exit," I say, meaning the underground tunnel that runs from my basement to an alley two blocks away behind the Malibu Tanning Salon, where Selia parks her car.

"I wish you'd quit," she says. She puts on her jacket. "Then maybe, after six months or so when everyone didn't hate you so much anymore, we could just spend time together like a normal couple. Go to dinner at Primo's. Maybe take in a movie without having to drive to New Hampshire."

"Hon, I can't quit," I say. "No more than you can quit taking care of your mother. These people need me."

"Eff them," she says. "They need *someone*. Not you specifically. There're other CAPPs."

I laugh. "It's not the sort of job that people are scrambling to fill."

"Fine, fine," she says, grabbing her handbag from the coffee table. She gives me a last peck on the lips. "Bye. Remember, you're my favorite little martyr."

I watch her disappear into the tunnel entrance and think, *I could say the same about you, hon, with your mother hanging around your neck like a leaden life preserver.* But that's not fair, really. Because like I said to her before, the sum total of adulthood is squelching the desire to run, screaming bloody goddamn murder, from the unpleasant things you're obliged to do. Selia's got her mom. I've got this town and the people in it.

But to keep moving forward, to remain faithful to those unpleasant things, everyone's got to reward themselves once in a while. I'm no exception. So I wait until I'm certain Selia's gone, then go to the safe in the bedroom and take out my vintage (not to mention illicit) collection of children's-clothing catalogs. There are forty-eight of them, everything from flimsy newspaper inserts to the collection's centerpiece, a glossy 700-page tome from BestDressedKids dating back to the Christmas before the adult population went gaga over children. Now, of course, children's-clothing catalogs—and the manufacture, distribution, or possession of them—are strictly forbidden, but with the money I make as CAPP I've been able to easily (if cautiously) acquire nearly fifty individual catalogs over the past year. Most come from Scandinavia, where there are few laws governing images of children, so the models have a noticeable blond-and-blue uniformity, but this is not a problem for me. Kids are kids.

I sit on the floor and spread out the collection in front of me.

For a while I savor the cover photos, the little arms and legs, the crisp new parkas and snappy denim overalls, the milk-tooth smiles. Then I gather the catalogs together in a stack and flip through each one. All my favorite pages I've marked with Post-it tabs. Each of my favorite children is a boy, each has a name and a story, and all their stories are happy ones. I smile and share the happiness as they revel in the satisfaction of normal lives and natural fibers. At times I'm so moved I cry a little.

But these are the only fantasies I allow myself. Though sometimes tempted, I never pretend that Laura is still alive, or that our son survived his birth and is now an adorable toddling gape-mouthed two-year-old, quick to giggle, with red hair like his mother's and a predilection for Mack truck worship. Never do I lie dozing on the sofa and imagine I hear his bare feet slapping across the kitchen floor in pursuit of a dust bunny or a Matchbox car. Nor do I fantasize about taking Selia, leaving this town to its miserable fate, and starting a family of our own in a warm, sane place.

Never, ever do I allow myself these luxuries.

No. After a while I gather up the catalogs, put them back in the safe, give the combination dial a spin, and go upstairs to put my dinner in the oven.

■

The next morning I need to go to the bank, so I leave home half an hour early. Lester Hicks, the president of Kennebec Federal Savings, has a six-year-old daughter and doesn't like me any more than any other parent, grandparent, godparent, aunt, uncle, big brother, or sister in town, but he grudgingly accepts my business on account of the fact that I'm worth more than the GNPs of Sierra Leone and Gambia combined.

This, of course, doesn't mean that they're pleasant or even polite to me there. When I reach the front of the line all three tellers simultaneously hang their NEXT WINDOW PLEASE signs and disappear. I wait. There's much grumbling in the line, not about the tellers, but about me. Someone calls into question my parentage, suggesting not so subtly that I am the product of bestiality. Another says I might be more sympathetic if I were a parent myself, but of course that would presuppose certain sexual functions of which I clearly am not capable. This goes on for fifteen minutes, until the tellers reappear, prodded from the break room by Lester. They argue with him in hushed, vicious tones. Finally Lester initiates several rounds of rock-paper-scissors, after which they return to their windows, the loser with her head hanging.

When I'm finished I head to the door and literally run into Selia walking in off the street.

"Hi," I say, knowing what's coming.

"Hi," she says quietly, then, louder: "Out of my way, jackass!" She screws up her face, hawks mightily, and spits a glob of phlegm onto my sports coat.

Everyone in the bank cheers. Selia gives me a look somewhere between amusement and apology. Though I know she'll deny it, I wonder if these "chance" meetings are something other than coincidence, as they seem to occur more frequently after we've had a disagreement. Selia being Selia, I wouldn't put it past her to manufacture a public encounter just so she'd have an excuse to abuse me a bit.

That night the only damage to the Celica is a gallon of red paint poured over the hood, so I get home from work a little early. Selia isn't there, and she doesn't show up until almost ten o'clock.

"Everything okay?" I ask when she comes in through the tunnel.

"Sorry," she says, throwing down her handbag. "I've been at the hospital all day. Mom got hold of a bag of potting soil from the shed and ate a heaping helping while I was at the bank. I found her in front of the TV, munching away, watching *The Price Is Right*."

"Well, gross, but what's the big deal? It's just dirt."

"No, it's that fortified stuff. Got all kinds of fertilizers and chemicals in it. They emptied her stomach and pumped her full of charcoal. Good news is, they're keeping her overnight, so I can stay here."

"Hey, great," I say, though I'm instantly disappointed, and a bit panicked, that I won't be able to go through my nightly routine with the catalogs.

Selia moves behind the sofa and kneads the muscles in my shoulders. "So I stuck around for a while and made sure they cleaned her hair and her nails and her dentures and changed her socks and let her keep the TV on because she can't sleep without it. Then, the other reason I'm so late, I had a flat tire when I came out of the hospital."

At this my ears prick up. "A flat? Was it slashed?"

"No," she says. "I had it towed to Arbo's, and they found a nail lodged in the tread. Said it happens all the time during the summer. Lots of construction, lots of nails lying about."

"Have you noticed Jeff Pauquette around anywhere?"

"I told you, it wasn't him," she says, rubbing harder. "Don't be so paranoid."

"Yeah, what am I worried about?" I say. "After that display of venom at the bank this morning, even if Jeff knew we were together no one would believe him."

Selia tries, not too hard, to stifle a titter. "Sorry about that," she says. "You have to admit, though, I was convincing."

"A little too convincing. That was my favorite coat."

"I'll pay to have it cleaned, big baby. Okay?"

"It's not the expense," I say. "It's having to drive all the way to the dry cleaner's in Dover."

"Oh, knock it off," Selia says. "I'll take your jacket to the cleaners. What else do I have to do? I'll drive. Mom would enjoy a little road trip."

Later, Selia wakes from a nightmare. She tells me she

dreamed she was driving to Dover and her mother grabbed my coat and leapt from the passenger seat, screaming some non-sense mantra about gefilte fish as she hit the pavement and rolled.

"I couldn't stop the car," Selia says. "I hit the brakes, but the car just kept going. And all I could think was, she wouldn't have been able to jump out if I'd paid the Adulation tax for child safety locks."

She's trembling.

"Try some milk," I suggest.

"Nah," she says. "I think I'll grab something a bit stronger from the bar, if you don't mind. First I'm going to call the hospital, though." She rises and heads for the stairs.

"Don't forget to disable the motion sensors," I call after her.

I wait until she's upstairs, then take the opportunity to sneak over to the safe and steal a few quick glances at BestDressed-Kids. When I hear Selia's footsteps returning I replace the catalog, close the safe door carefully so it won't make any noise, then hop back into bed.

■

The next day, Wednesday, my session with Jeff is scheduled for one in the afternoon. He shows up on time and actually smiles at me when I open the office door.

"How you doing, you?" he asks, bright and friendly.

"Fine, Jeff, thanks," I say. Jeff sits without being invited, and after a minute of staring quizzically at the back of his head, I take my seat behind the desk and set the timer for fifty minutes.

"Looks like they've left your car alone today, them," Jeff says. He's still smiling.

"Is that so?" I ask, trying to seem indifferent. "If you had to venture a guess, would you say the chances are good they'll continue to leave it alone?"

Jeff makes a show of considering this. He tilts his head back and rubs his stubbled chin thoughtfully. "Yeah," he says. "They're in a real good mood today, them, so I think your car will be fine."

"Well, that's great news," I say.

"Maybe not." He stares, giving me the biggest smile yet. For a moment I'm certain my life is about to end, suddenly and with great violence; Jeff's finally lost it and is going to brain me with the official CAPA paperweight, a statuette of a smiling child with the words NOTHING SPECIAL stamped upon its base. I look away, chilled. When I look back he's still staring, still smiling, but it's not violence I read in his eyes. Rather, his expression is that of a five-card-stud player sitting on three aces.

I clear my throat and shuffle some papers on the desk. "Well, let's get to it, Jeff," I say. "I'd planned a session of negative-image negative-reinforcement today, so if you'll just take off your shirt so I can affix the electrodes . . ."

"Sure thing." He unbuttons his flannel and slips it off. Four hairless spots remain on his chest from our last NINR session. When I come around the desk with the electrodes, Jeff takes them from my hand and sticks them on himself.

"All set, me," he says, smoothing the adhesive circles with the tips of his fingers. He looks up and smiles some more.

I take my seat again and turn on the machine. "Ready?"

"Fire away," he says.

I show Jeff a picture of his son Abe.

"Mama's boy. Too sensitive. Bad fisherman. Can't even stand to put a hook through a goddamn worm. A sissy, him."

"Good," I say. My hand hovers, eager and trembling, over the shock toggle switch. "More."

"Ugly. Gap-toothed. One eye bigger than the other. And that harelip you're always going on about, you. Still gives me the willies to look at it. Kid looks like a big bald cat."

We continue. I stretch the session ten minutes beyond the customary half hour, putting Jeff through his paces, covering both Abe and his other son Corey, as well as negative impressions of children in general. Jeff requires correction only once, when he criticizes Abe for not caring what the kids at school think of him. I press the toggle switch for somewhat longer than the prescribed two seconds, then tell him this is a tricky one but that what children think is so utterly irrelevant that not even other children should pay it any heed.

I am, admittedly, disappointed that I don't have another opportunity to correct him.

"That wasn't too bad," he says as I remove the electrodes and hand him his flannel. "Did pretty good, me."

"You're all set for this week, Jeff," I say. "I suppose you can see yourself out."

"Suppose I can," he says, rising from the chair.

"You're sure they're going to leave my car alone, right?"

"The car, it's safe," he says. "Those fellows who beat up your car, they're happy as clams today, them."

Finally, like a big, dumb fish, I bite. "Why, Jeff?" I ask. "What is it that's got them in such a great mood?"

He pauses at the door. "Let me answer your question with a question," he says. "I wonder, how much of the big bucks you make running down our kids did it cost you to build that tunnel, anyhow?"

We stare at each other. My mouth hangs open, and I can't seem to close it.

"Later, boss," Jeff says, smiling again as he closes the door behind him.

■

Selia calls me in a panic.

"My car is destroyed," she says. "All the windows are broken. It looks like someone took a chain saw to the tires."

"It's Jeff," I say.

"No shit it's Jeff," she says. "How did he find out about us?"

"I have no idea. He knows about the tunnel. He must have seen you coming or going."

"Jesus."

"Selia, calm down," I say.

"I will not calm down! What am I going to do? I'll end up like you, driving sixty miles to get a Pepsi."

"Honey," I say, "we'll figure something out."

"He'll tell everyone. And they'll tell everyone else. They'll run me out of town. They'll show up at my house with torches and a rope," she says. "I can't leave here. Mom would die. She grew up in that house."

"It might not be that bad."

"Don't say that," she says. "You know better. It will be very, very bad. It will be the worst."

She starts to cry. Like a stone I sit there with the handset pressed against my ear, listening to her sobs, and gradually I become what I have not been for a very long time—angry.

"Don't take this the wrong way," she says quietly, "because it's really no reflection on you, but at the moment I'm sort of sorry we ever met. I feel like I should say that."

My mind, spurred by an anger so sudden and unfamiliar, gallops furiously ahead, and I barely hear her.

"I think that's the hardest thing about God being dead," Selia says. "You know? Because before, when bad things happened, you could always shake your fist at the sky and say something nasty under your breath and you kind of knew that God would understand, he put you in a shit situation, so you had a right to be pissed. Now, things go sour and there's no one to take the blame."

"Selia," I say. "Get your mother together. I'll come pick you up."

"Where are we going?"

"The Grand Asian Buffet."

There's a pause on her end. "What?"

"Just listen to me," I say. "I've got an idea."

Selia listens. When I'm finished she cries some more and says she won't do it, no way, no how, but her refusal is of the impotent variety offered by those who realize they have no other choice.

"I'll be ready in ten," she sniffles.

■

Despite regular outbreaks of food poisoning, the Grand Asian Buffet has been Watertown's most popular restaurant six years running. It's also the only place in town where I'm allowed to sit down to a meal, as the owner, Ping, being Chinese, possesses an attitude toward children of dutiful indifference, and so isn't required to attend my therapy sessions.

When we arrive the parking lot is, as always, full. I put the Jaguar in park and turn to Selia.

"Okay," I say. "I'm going in. Wait here fifteen minutes or so, then come in and do your thing."

Selia won't look at me. "I hate this," she says. "I hate you for making me do it."

"There's not much else we can do," I say. "Unless you want to move to New Hampshire."

"I'm not going to New Hampshire," Selia's mother says from the backseat.

"Okay?" I say. "Selia?"

"Okay."

"You've got to sell it," I tell her. "You've got to be utterly convincing for this to work."

"Betty?" her mother says. "Where are you taking me?"

"We're going to have some dinner, Ma," Selia says.

I get out of the car and enter the restaurant through fiberglass doors decorated to resemble the gates of a feudal Chinese fortress. The cavernous dining room is full. Two hundred faces turn, stare, and darken. The Shofner family, on seeing me, rise and stalk out, leaving behind half-eaten plates of food. Ping, smiling modestly, leads me to a table near the scale replica of the Great Wall which runs the length of the restaurant.

"Something to drink?" he asks.

"How about a Heineken," I say.

"Of course." He motions toward the buffet at the end of the dining room. "You may help yourself."

And though I'm not hungry I think, why not? This will be the last time for a while that I'll be able to partake of fried rice and wontons. So I run the gauntlet of grumbling diners. Selia's name curls off their acid lips. When I reach the buffet everyone else clears out except for a boy of fourteen or so wearing a T-shirt that reads: I HAVE THE DICK, SO I MAKE THE RULES.

I head back to my table after heaping up a plate and spot Jeff sitting with his family against the far wall. He smiles and waves. I put a thumb into my mouth and puff out my cheeks as though I'm blowing up a balloon. I raise my middle finger slowly until it's fully "inflated," then display it to Jeff. He just keeps smiling.

I'm into my second plate and third beer when the doors open, setting off a crash of gongs through the PA speakers. Selia enters with her mother in tow, and the entire restaurant goes silent as the gongs fade.

Selia calls for attention, but she's already got it.

"By now, many of you know I've been spending time with this man." She points at me. "I can imagine what you must think. You consider me a traitor, a whore, an all-around bad citizen. What you don't know, however, is that my aim was not to consort with this filth, but to rid our community of him. Now, finally, I have the means to do so."

Not angry enough, I think. Not disdainful enough. Sell it, honey. Sell it.

"Before coming here today, I placed a call to the Kennebec County sheriff's office," she continues. "As we speak, deputies are searching his home. In his home they will find a safe. And in that safe they will find a large, carefully annotated, and totally illegal cache of children's clothing catalogs."

A murmur ripples through the diners. Selia's got one more

block of dialogue to get through, an exclamation point of derision about me being a hypocrite and a child worshipper. But her eyes have begun to well with tears, and I jump in before she blows the whole thing. I rise from the table, mustering an expression of wounded betrayal.

"Selia," I say. "How could you do this?"

She looks at me. Her eyes shimmer. For a horrible moment I think she's going to break down and embrace me, but then her face goes dark with an anger as real and implacable as death.

"Shut your mouth, you son of a bitch." She rears back and kicks me squarely in the balls. I go down like a sack of bricks, utterly convinced.

The restaurant is silent.

"Betty," Selia's mother says, tugging her hand. "Betty. They've got beef and broccoli. Can we have beef and broccoli?"

·

Prison isn't nearly as bad as we're led by prosecutors and newsmagazines to believe. At least not the prison they've sent me to, a minimum security compound in the midcoast region. No shanks or forced sex here. My fellow convicts are all nonviolent offenders, largely white-collar sane individuals who can be trusted with a knife, if not your wallet. I eat well. I can come and go more or less as I please within the compound. There's cable television, and movies in the rec room on Tuesday and Saturday nights. In the yard we play volleyball, basketball, horseshoes. Once a week five or six of us gather in the quad for poker. I've got gratifying work as a peer counselor, helping other inmates cope with depression, sexual privation, and the guilt associated with having disappointed and shamed their families.

I'd almost forgotten how it feels to be liked.

Still, until very recently something was bothering me, a gray malaise which kept me up nights staring at the springs on the underside of the top bunk, or else caused me to drift away when I should have been listening to a fellow inmate in my care. For a while I thought it was simply that I missed Selia, but when I projected my thoughts into the future and imagined the time, not too distant from now, when we'd be reunited, it did little to help me feel better. After months of sleepless nights I was able to identify this discomfort only as a desire. Far from lifting the cloud, however, this realization served only to darken it—now that I knew I longed for something, I wanted desperately to know what that something was.

And then, just yesterday, this letter from Selia:

Only a year left. It'll go by before we know it, and then we can leave this shitass town and get on with our lives. So I've got a proposal—and brace yourself, because it's a whopper—but since Mom died I've been really lonely for someone to care for. Ridiculous, sure, but there it is. So here's what I'm thinking: you, me, a bambino. We're different from the fawning retards around here. We'll be good, sensible parents. And we'd make a good-looking kid, too, as long as he didn't end up with your nose. I've thought about it for a while, and I know this is what I want. So I'm going to Dr. DerSimonian next week to have my IUD removed. And just think, you'll never have to wear a rubber again! Small consolation, I know, when you're still a year away from getting laid. But maybe the thought will keep you warm nights.

I read the letter three, four times. I put it down on the desk and read it again, lacing and unlacing my fingers. My palms went cold with sweat; I wiped them on the canvas of my prison-issue pantlegs as my breath came quicker and I longed for a cigarette though I've never smoked, and then, with trembling hands, I took out pen and paper and wrote my response, one word, three letters, in a bold, capital script which took up the whole page: YES.

Grace

Look not thou upon the wine when it is red, when it giveth his colour in the cup, when it moveth itself aright. At the last it biteth like a serpent, and stingeth like an adder. Yea, thou shalt be as he that lieth down in the midst of the sea, or as he that lieth upon the top of a mast. They have stricken me, shalt thou say, and I was not sick; they have beaten me, and I felt it not: when shall I awake? I will seek it yet again.

—Proverbs 23:31–32; 34–35

I'm riding with my father in his truck when I see the kid, lying motionless in the grass, his head resting below a window of the house he's crawled up against. There's a backpack there, and a crappy old ten-speed that's been half-propped, half-crashed against a tree.

"There's a kid hurt over there," I say to my father. We've been mowing lawns, so he doesn't have his hearing aids in, and I have to repeat myself. By the time he understands what I'm saying we're already past and down the hill. My father makes a wide turn, swinging the trailer around, and heads back.

We pull up in front of the house and get out. As we cross the lawn I see that the figure lying there is not a kid, but a grown man. He looks a little younger than my father, late forties maybe. He's lying on his side; the seat of his jeans is soiled with either dirt or shit, I can't tell. There's a Bud Ice bottle on the ground near his head, empty except for a bit of yellowish foam in the bottom, and a busted-up placard that reads GOD LIVES. The man's eyes are half-open and staring. He might be dead.

I'm always thinking the worst.

To be on the safe side I let my father take the lead. He just retired from thirty years as a paramedic, so he knows better than I do how to deal with this.

We stand over the man, and my father says, "Hey." He takes the man's arm at the elbow. "Hey," he says, shaking him. "Wake up, buddy."

"His name's Lou," someone says.

A woman's face appears behind the window screen. My father looks at me; he thinks I said something. I point to the woman.

"His name's Lou," she says again, to my father.

"What's that?" my father asks.

"Lou," she half-yells.

"Hey Lou," my father says. He takes Lou's wrist between his fingers, counting the pulse against the second hand on his watch. "You know him?" he asks the woman.

She gives a bitter smile. "That's one way to put it," she says. "I wouldn't let him in."

"Does he have any medical problems? He diabetic?"

"He's drunk," the woman says.

My father places Lou's hand back on the ground, then loosens the shirt around Lou's neck, to let him breathe. Lou starts to snore. He sounds like an angry rattlesnake.

I stand there, rubbing the grit on the back of my neck, staring down at Lou, thinking.

"You should call the police," my father says to the woman.

"He's just drunk," she says.

"What?"

She repeats herself, louder.

"Call the police," my father says. "Tell them to send an ambulance. It's better that he go to the hospital. He can't be left out here in this heat."

The woman stands at the window a moment longer, then disappears into the darkness of the house. After a while she comes back.

"They're on their way," she says.

My father is looking down at Lou and doesn't hear her.

"Okay," I tell the woman.

"I'm going to shut the window."

"We'll stay out here until they come," I say. She closes the window, glances once more at Lou, then disappears again.

■

My father and I stand with our hands on our hips, squinting in the sunlight. I kick at the grass, shifting my gaze around, trying not to look at Lou. My father bends over to check his pulse again.

Then my father says, "Kind of reminds you why you quit, huh?" He doesn't look at me when he says it.

For a minute I don't respond. Then I say, "I started drinking again a year ago."

He looks up. "Hm?" he says.

"I said, 'That's no way to live.'" I form the words carefully so he can understand.

■

Eventually the cop shows up. He's short and thick and has a crew cut. He knows Lou, but calls him Preacher.

"One of your regulars?" my father asks.

"Oh yeah," the cop says. "We've been looking for him today." He and my father laugh knowingly. I don't laugh. Instead, I set my lips in a straight line against the front of my teeth. The two of them crouch on either side of Lou, colleagues now.

"I don't like his breathing," the cop says.

"Yeah, his breathing's good," my father says. "His pulse is a little weak."

The cop looks at my father for a minute, then reaches in and squeezes Lou's nipple through his shirt. "Come on, Preacher. Wake up, buddy." But Lou doesn't move.

"You got an ambulance coming?" my father says.

"Yeah. I can take it from here."

"Okay," my father says. He straightens up, stretches a bit. "We've got more work to do anyway."

We start back toward the truck, and the cop says, "Thanks for your help, guys." I've got my back to him, and I jump when he says it. It sounds funny: *guys,* addressing both of us, though I haven't said a word, haven't been a help to anyone.

My father turns at the waist and raises his hand. I keep walking, and don't look back.

I haven't thought of you in what seems like a long time, but for some reason I do now. I see you knocking bottles off the coffee table with an angry sweep of your arm. I hear your voice from behind a locked door, screaming there's no God, why can't I just accept it like everyone else? I picture you crying so hard and so long your eyes swell shut. I wonder where you are, who you're with, if you flinch every time he moves his hands, like you did with me.

Interview with the Last Remaining Member of the Feral Dog Pack Which Fed on God's Corpse

And he said unto them, Unto you it is given to know the mystery of the kingdom of God: but unto them that are without, all *these* things are done in parables: That seeing they may see, and not perceive; and hearing they may hear, and not understand; lest at any time they should be converted, and *their* sins should be forgiven them.

—Mark 4:11–12

Author's Note: Interview conducted in the Sudanese desert, near the town of Nertiti, in early June 2006. After five months of searching Southern Darfur for _____, who by then had already passed out of any verifiable contact with people, I'd set out for Nertiti from Nyala, but managed to travel only seventy kilometers before the jeep I'd purchased for the trip bogged down in a sand lake. I didn't last much longer than the truck. Lost and disoriented, to escape the heat I crawled into an abandoned animal den. With no idea where I was in relation to Nertiti, and no strength to get there even if I'd known the way, I assumed I would die. It was at dusk on the second day that _____entered the den, and the interview began.

It should be noted that this interview took place through extrasensory means; that is, _____ and I communicated without either of us actually speaking. Also, owing to my burgeoning delirium, many of the questions I put forth to _____were more or less nonsensical (though he was able to intuit what I was asking and answer accordingly). For the sake of readability I represent those questions here with the simple device of an uppercase bold **Q**. The substance of the queries can, for the most part, be inferred from _____'s responses.

My absolute recall of the interview, as well as my eventual emergence from the den and arrival in Nertiti, less than half a kilometer away, can only be attributed to some intervention on _____'s part, the nature of which I won't pretend to understand.

—RFC

Q?

Locating you was fairly simple, really, and has less to do with whatever abilities I gained from eating the Creator than with the abilities I already possessed as a feral dog. Contrary to what people believe, I'm far from omniscient. There are huge gaps in my knowledge of things, as I presume was the case for our Creator. For example, I was aware that you sought me out, and I knew you were somewhere in Darfur, but beyond that I was more or less in the dark. Among dogs, though, those of us with the best noses can detect the smell of a dying animal at ridiculous distances. Despair, like its cousin fear, carries a bitter scent, and just a few molecules of it, driven across the plains on a gusty afternoon, are more than enough for me to trace its source. Finding you was not difficult at all.

Q?

No. I'd expend more calories in the effort of chewing you than I would gain. Too thickly muscled. The inevitable result of obsessive weight lifting. So please, don't worry; though you'd make an easy meal, easy meals are plentiful for us during the hot season. I'm sated. But that's not the only reason I won't eat you.

Q?

Oh, this whole application-of-morality-to-animal-behavior problem I've been grappling with since eating the Creator. Compassion is a coat of fur I find particularly ill-fitting. Just doesn't mesh well with the nature of a dog. To feel pity for the young, old, weak, injured, and infirm—and as a result to abstain from killing them—not only contradicts that which is feral dog directive number one, but also is poor strategy from the standpoint of self-preservation. I'm still in the early stages of sorting it all out, and honestly it often makes me unhappy.

Then there's a third reason I won't eat you—much as I desire now to avoid your kind, I do sometimes miss intelligent company. This is why I'm here.

Q?

Don't be silly—yes, even by my lofty standards you are intelligent. If I may be frank, this was one of the things that eventually repulsed me about people. The way they prostrated themselves before me, sometimes literally, with hands clasped and all manner of entreaty on their lips, but more often figuratively, as you do now—"My meager intellect can't possibly compare with yours," et cetera, ad nauseam. One shouldn't confuse knowledge with intelligence. Is an encyclopedia smarter than you? Or a computer?

Q.

Of course not. So what makes you so certain that I am? The fact that I know without having been there what India's Prime Minister, Dr. Manmohan Singh, ate for dinner last night? I do. He had a bit of a sour stomach, and so ate a bland mixture of lentils and rice, of which he finished only a meager portion. There. Can you accept this, and still be my friend? Not my supplicant, not my apostle, but my friend?

Q?

It does. It does upset me. From the perspective of one steeped in the social customs of dogs, the eagerness with which people bow down, with little prompting and no real evidence that such humility and reverence are justified, is beyond distasteful. Especially when, as I'm now aware, that humility obscures a greed and sense of entitlement which is nearly ubiquitous in your kind. Boundless duplicity. It's small wonder great masses of you are so unhappy.

So, to sum up: You're smarter than the average wildebeest. Which will suffice.

Q?

Yes, perhaps it would be better to change the subject.

Q?

Certainly I'm willing to talk about it. You've nearly killed yourself for the dubious privilege of hearing my story, after all. Where should I begin?

Q.

Well, I think I should start a bit *before* the beginning, because it seems worth mentioning that I and another dog had an encounter with the Creator a few days before the five of us actually ate him. An odd coincidence, in retrospect. I can't offer much detail, because my recollection of life before my transformation is vague, and could probably be more accurately described as a general impression of experience, rather than memories in the sense that I've come to know them.

It was around this time of year. I know this for certain, because the days were searing hot. Dogs are not terribly intelligent, but they are very good at finding food, and we'd learned from our mothers, who had learned from their mothers, and so on, to follow the roving bands of Janjaweed militia, because food was always plentiful in their wake. They killed everything in a village, and when they moved on to find more to kill, we came in and cleaned up after them. A tidy relationship, except for the rare occasion when one or two of us neglected to keep a safe distance from the Janjaweed and found ourselves in their path. The first time I encountered the Creator, this was what happened. My brother and I caught the scent of despair and, unwisely, we followed it, ranging ahead of the Janjaweed until we found a young woman lying half-conscious and alone in the tall grass. I did not know at the time that this was the Creator, in the form of a Dinka woman. I had no capacity to understand the concept, of course. All I saw was an easy meal. We walked cautious circles around her, to test her awareness and ability to fight. She did not strike out, did not flail or cry or respond at all, and we were about to make the kill when we heard the Janjaweed drawing near. Without hesitation, we bolted. This was our only hope for survival. They can't be outrun, and believe me when I say that whatever they come into contact with dies.

Q?

Well, after that my brother and I returned to the pack and resolved, insofar as dogs are capable of resolving, that it was better to be hungry and alive than full and dead. We knew that with the Janjaweed on the move, our patience would be rewarded. Two days later we followed the smell of scorched flesh to the ruins of the refugee camp. This was when the five of us, those famous five, partook of the Creator.

Q?

That strikes me as a tactless question, not to mention beside the point.

Q.

I suppose you're right; it is rare information. I can see why you'd be curious, however morbid that curiosity may be.

Q?

Fine, I'll indulge you. It was tough, sour, gritty, the vilest meat I've ever tasted. Which was why none of us ate more than a mouthful.

Q.

It is surprising, when one stops to think about it. The flavor was anything but divine.

Q?

No. I don't recall my transformation. There is a gap in my memory between the last moments as the dog I'd always been—wild, cheerful, nothing more or less than the sum of my appetites—and this new, heightened sentience. But I can tell you it was not instantaneous. When we discussed the sequence of events later, the others confirmed that their experience of the change was identical. For several hours after eating the Creator, we continued to feed at the refugee camp with the rest of the pack. Eventually we came together and moved west out of the camp to find a suitable place to spend the night. These, now, were the last moments of my old life. I tramped down a bed in the tall grass and set about grooming myself. I lapped at my paws until the bloody paste was gone from between my toes, then used the pads to wipe away the crust of blood on my snout. I was surrounded by the nighttime noises of my brothers and sisters and cousins and uncles, rolling languidly onto their backs, sighing and growling in pleasant fatigue from the long day of eating. Soon the satisfaction of a full stomach, combined with a cool north wind blowing steadily over my fur, lulled me to sleep.

I did not dream.

The next morning I woke to the sun glaring down from a throne of distant hills. Immediately I was aware of the change I'd undergone. Whereas before I'd known only impulse, instinct, and habit, now suddenly my mind was full of thoughts; whereas before nothing existed for me outside of what I could detect with my senses, now I could apprehend the whole earth as a single entity, the minute and varied ways in which the parts of this whole interacted, passed into and out of being. All this became clear and accessible in a flash of consciousness, and with the same clarity I realized that my time as a member of the pack had come to an end.

The other four had reached this same conclusion. Our departure was as natural and inevitable as the sunrise. We rose together and prepared slowly to leave, hobbled by the unfamiliar complexity of sorrow. Hearing us, my brother stirred. He shook briskly to wake himself and trotted over, wanting to come along, thinking perhaps we meant to do some early scavenging before the day grew too hot. I tried to tell him that he couldn't accompany us, but already the old way of communicating seemed lost to me. I flattened my ears when I should have brushed shoulders with him; I raised my tail when I should have lowered my snout. Frustrated, I showed him my teeth, and he moved away one small backward step at a time, tail drooping, eyes meek and downcast.

I haven't seen him since that day, and of all the sorrows that

I've learned, this last image of him is among those that pain me the most.

Q?

No. I'm aware, in my way, that he's doing well—happy, healthy, a father now. Loss, among our kind, is a daily fact of life, and he forgot about me almost as soon as I disappeared from sight. My sadness is for myself.

Q?

Much as I would like to, I can't seek him out, for the same reason I had to leave the pack that day—I don't belong anymore. I never will again. I don't expect you to understand this. You're not equipped to understand it.

Q?

We had no specific destination in mind when we left. We did know that people, in addition to being both our most plentiful food and our most dangerous enemy, possessed great intelligence. We hoped we might find a new home among them. So we headed toward the large cities of the north, but the going was hard. With the knowledge of time, our legs were heavy with regret and dread. None of us could muster the spirit to hunt. We passed hungry through great plains and dry riverbeds, up and over hills, across dark stretches of desert. At night we tried to comfort ourselves in the old ways, by grooming one another and curling together while we slept, but these things were empty now, useless as wings on a chicken.

Finally we came to an oasis farming village. With new hope we approached the first person we saw, a thin old man with a long, gently seamed face. I asked him, in the same way you and I are communicating now, if he could take us to the person in charge of the village.

Only four of us left that place alive, running as fast as our weakened legs would carry us. The one who did not survive lay in the dust of the village's single road, a rifle bullet in his head. The farmers, as Christians, believed we were evil spirits rather than dogs, and they pursued us into the desert with their guns. We escaped into a system of underground caves and spent three days and nights inside, mourning our friend and our fate. Snouts on paws, we whimpered in the gloom and dust; we still knew how to do this, at least, and it was the same waste of time it had always been.

Q?

It's a good question. I've tried many times to explain this to people, without much success. The analogy I use, when comparing a normal dog's emotional range to that of a person, is the difference between primary colors and the wide gamut of secondary colors. Normal dogs, for example, will experience a primal anger—let's call it basic red. People, on the other hand, have an entire spectrum of red shades—the scarlet of irritation, the vermilion of resentment, the deep crimson of fury, and so on. The four of us now possessed this emotional kaleidoscope— or it possessed us—and early on, the strain of enduring it nearly drove us insane.

Q?

We might have died there if it hadn't occurred to us, for the first time, to talk to one another. To use our new knowledge, share our thoughts and figure out a potential solution. This was our third night in the caves. With an enthusiasm that in our former lives had been reserved only for stalking prey or mating, we cast our minds further north, searching for the right person to reveal ourselves to, a person with intelligence, learning, and an intellectual curiosity that would allow him to get past the initial shock of being spoken to by a dog. After several hours we decided on Khalid Hassan Mubarak, a professor of theology at the University of Khartoum. Mubarak kept up appearances as a pious Muslim for professional reasons, but years before had jettisoned all religious conviction to make way for an innate and blossoming egomania. In our zeal and naïveté we neglected to consider Mubarak's character as well as his intellect, a mistake we would all come to regret.

Q?

We were anxious to get under way, so we returned to the oasis while the village still slept, and drank from the spring pool until our guts bloated like water skins. We headed northeast, trotting a straight line to Khartoum, again over hills and across great stretches of sand, pausing only for an hour or two each day when the sun rose to its apex and beat every living thing into hiding. We hunted without much success; though all of us had been accomplished predators before, now we stalked like pups, clumsily and with little teamwork, managing only to kill an old plated lizard none of us had much interest in eating. But not even hunger could dampen our optimism or slow our pace, and soon Khartoum's slender minarets rose from the desert like a miracle.

Q?

No, I don't believe in miracles, not in the way I think you mean it. Sorry to disappoint. I never had an opportunity to believe. One moment I was ignorant of the very concept of miracles, and the next I knew far too much to believe them possible. I use the word as a figure of speech, to describe the shock of seeing this huge city materialize out of nothing but wind and sand.

Q?

What can I say, really, about my first impressions of Khartoum? It goes without saying that none of us had seen anything like it before. The noise and bustle. The people packed together, shouting and grabbing at sleeves, demanding the attention of others but never offering their own. The broken, bullet-pocked cars jockeying endlessly for position. The riot of the bazaars, the stink of rotting fish and apple shisha, the vacant stares of loitering war-wounded. We became lost as if in a sandstorm, unnoticed except when a soldier or shopkeeper kicked at us. We scurried through the streets for most of the afternoon until we arrived, more or less by accident, at the campus of the university.

Q?

We waited outside the building where we knew Mubarak lectured. After an hour he emerged, tall and pale in a plain white dishdasha and embroidered skullcap. I approached him and, for lack of any suitable entrée, said simply "Hello."

Q.

It was somewhat absurd, but there seemed no reasonable way for us to introduce ourselves.

Q?

Well, as you can imagine, Mubarak was taken aback. At first he didn't notice me at all, and looked around to see who had spoken. The only other person on the common, a man in a crimson tunic, had his back to Mubarak and was well out of earshot besides, receding around the corner of the Agriculture building.

"Down here," I said. "At your feet."

Mubarak looked down and, seeing me, muttered a reflexive curse to a God he no longer believed in.

"Professor Mubarak," I said, flanked now by the others, "we've come to ask for your help."

"Have I gone mad?"

"No," I said. "I don't think so. I'm speaking, in a manner of speaking, and you're hearing me. This is real."

Mubarak was silent for a few moments, staring down at us. Absently he put a hand to his skullcap and adjusted it. "What . . . ?" he said, his voice trailing off, but already we could sense his disbelief waning a bit, giving way to the intellectual vitality with which he'd mastered seven languages and established himself as one of the leading translators of the Qur'an. I saw this opportunity and seized it, rushing headlong into an explanation: the Janjaweed, the refugee camp—

But Mubarak interrupted me. "Not here," he said, still seemingly dazed. "Whether this is real or not, I can't be talking to dogs in public for everyone to see. I'm walking home. Follow me—at a distance."

So we did. Mubarak left the campus and headed east, and we trailed him, thrilled at the possibility, so close now that we'd found our ambassador, the one who would introduce us to the world of people and help us belong somewhere again. In our excitement we failed to notice Mubarak duck into a grocery stall to buy a pack of Dunhills. Without realizing it we passed him and reached his home before he did; we were waiting outside the gate when he arrived.

"How did you know where I live?" he asked.

"We'll explain everything," I told him. "Insofar as we understand it."

Q?

We went inside and told him our story. Mubarak listened and chain-smoked. An amused little smile played beneath his mustache, as if he had accepted that none of this was real and decided to have fun with it, to hear us out and discover the fine points of his madness. Even the air he breathed, heavy with tobacco smoke and spices from the shwarma stand beneath his window, was suspect.

"Right now I could smoke a thousand of these without consequence," he said, holding up a freshly lit cigarette. "Because none of this is actually happening."

"Professor," I said, "we understand that you want to believe that's the case. That you need to believe it, because in your mind there are only two logical explanations for what is happening— either you're dreaming, or you're insane. But we assure you that this is very real."

Mubarak absorbed this in silence, then suddenly rose and stalked out, leaving us alone in the apartment. He returned several minutes later with a sodden package of chicken livers wrapped in newsprint. The mischievous smile was gone from his face.

"You must be starved," he said, gazing down on us warmly.

Q?

For three days we fattened up on raw liver and goat's milk, and slept on woven rugs. Mubarak bathed and brushed us, switched on ceiling fans and drew the curtains to shut out the afternoon sun. In the perpetual twilight of the living room, we dozed and were thankful. For the first time, I licked a man's hand in affection.

Still, despite the luxury we were restless, and when we asked when he would introduce us to the larger world, Mubarak told us soon, soon, but first we would have to return to the refugee camp. He said that for practical reasons only I could accompany him; the others would have to stay behind at his apartment. He took leave from the university and quickly made plans for an expedition south. This was also when he introduced the cages, stainless-steel kennels padlocked from the outside, which he said were for our protection and comfort. When not in the kennels we would need to be leashed, again for our own protection.

Mubarak purchased a used Land Rover, loaded it with gas canisters, food, water, and several body bags purchased from a man he knew who trafficked in illicit arms, and off we went. He worried aloud that the rains would arrive early and turn the roads to impassable mud holes; as a consequence we traveled faster than was safe and arrived at the camp in just three days, having used both the spare tires. Small groups of aid workers had returned and were busy cleaning up the dismembered, putrefying corpses. Mubarak cursed when he saw them.

"They haven't retrieved the Creator's remains yet," I assured him.

"Where?" he said. "Show me. Quickly."

We rolled through the collection of makeshift shelters, most of them knocked flat or burned to cinders, past the communal well, and out to the edge of the camp, where we found the Creator's body exactly as we had left it three weeks earlier.

"There," I said.

Mubarak put the truck in neutral and engaged the parking brake. "It hasn't decayed at all," he said, and he was right. The Creator was dead, certainly, and picked over, but while the other corpses were so badly decomposed they'd begun to liquefy in places, his flesh was still fresh and supple, as if he'd died only a few hours before.

Without another word Mubarak leapt from the truck and began stuffing the body in one of the black vinyl bags. He moved hurriedly, continuing without pause even as he gagged on the almost visible stench that hung in the air. An aid worker, standing amidst a group of corpses perhaps fifty feet away, called out in muffled English through his respirator: "You! What are you doing?" The bag protruded here and there with hastily packed knees and elbows, and Mubarak gave up trying to zip it as the worker and two others approached. Instead he dragged the body to the back of the truck and heaved it inside, then clambered into the driver's seat and jammed the accelerator even before he'd closed his door.

The aid workers ran to stop us, but a cloud of yellow dust kicked up by the wheels enveloped them, and they disappeared from sight as we sped away. Mubarak kept the accelerator to the floor until the camp had melted into the horizon behind us. Then, suddenly, he stopped the truck, got out, and went around to the back again.

I knew what he meant to do.

"This may not be a good idea," I told him, but already he had the tailgate down and was pulling a jackknife from the breast pocket of his khaki vest.

"Shut up," he said. He raised his eyes to mine; gone, suddenly, was the benevolence he had shown us, replaced by something base and sinister, something frightening even to my predator's heart. "If you lied to me . . ."

The Creator's hand, pale palm up, hung from the opening of the bag, and Mubarak seized it by the thumb and cut away a bloodless chunk of flesh with the knife. He hesitated, pausing just before the meat touched his lips. I saw that his fingers were trembling. Then he bit down hard, as if eating something that might bite back. Eyes closed, he chewed quickly and had to throw his head back to swallow.

When he opened his eyes again he gazed about like someone emerging into light, expectant and wondering, but soon realized that nothing had changed in either him or the way he perceived his surroundings. Disappointment crossed his face, then anger. He slammed the tailgate shut and climbed back into the driver's seat.

"You made a cannibal of me, for nothing," he said.

"Professor," I said, "we told you that the change would take time." I considered pointing out that I had advised against his eating the Creator, but thought better of it.

In any event, he had stopped listening. He turned the truck around and headed north again, making an off-road detour around the refugee camp. We drove in silence until night fell, when Mubarak pulled off, reclined the seat, and fell asleep with his arms folded across his chest.

Q?

Quite simply, in the morning he was changed, just as we had been. Mubarak didn't speak of it—not one word—but it was obvious. Whatever he gained (and this I never determined, as our time together was drawing to a close and I would not see him alive again), he seemed mostly to be hobbled by the transformation in strange and inexplicable ways. For one thing, he had difficulty driving: grinding gears, pressing the gas when brakes were indicated and vice versa, and failing to notice turns in the road. More than once he got stuck on the soft shoulder and had to use a hand winch to free the truck. When he spoke, which was not often, he peppered his sentences with words that did not belong and which he did not seem to notice coming out of his mouth. For example, at one point he said, "I must call Ibrahim and make plans pedagogical to move the body to London."

"What?" I said. "Professor, are you all right?"

"Shut up. I wasn't talking to you. I'm just thinking thimbleful out loud."

And so on. Needless to say, it was an odd and somewhat frightening ride back to Khartoum, because not only was Mubarak acting strangely, but it was becoming clear that though we'd trusted him, allowed ourselves to be locked up in steel cages, he had no intention of helping us join human society.

Q?

He did nothing to us, strictly speaking. When we arrived in Khartoum he simply put me in the spare room with the others. The next day he left for London, taking the Creator's body with him and leaving us behind, still in the cages. The others had had no food or water for six days. Their ribs showed through their fur, and the skin of their noses was dried and cracked. They pressed into the corners of the cages, trying vainly to distance themselves from their own feces.

Q?

I can only assume he meant for us to die there in his apartment. At the time it saddened me to reach this conclusion. This is, again, one of the great moral chasms between your kind and mine. Among dogs, one does not use affection to deceive, as Mubarak did. It simply doesn't happen. So when I realized he'd departed without giving a thought to us, I was confused. I wondered what we had done wrong; surely the blame rested with us, somehow. Even now, though I'm much wiser, it still hurts to think that he left us there to starve.

Q?

We grieved, for everything we'd lost and were about to lose. For dogs, to grieve means to howl, and so we did, through that first night and into the next day. The others' voices weakened, then dropped out of the chorus altogether, and soon I was alone, crying out against the walls of that room, throwing myself headlong into the bars of the cage until my snout was bloodied, feeling my insides shrivel and fail.

Q?

What happened to Mubarak is well documented; you probably know as much as I do. In London he met with Ibrahim Hussein Al-Jamil, a friend and colleague who lectured at King's College. Together they oversaw the autopsy and study of the Creator's corpse, which revealed, among other things, a massless composition that defied long-held principles of physics. A select group of scientists descended on London, all of whom agreed, on reaching the inevitable conclusion, that it must be kept from the public. Mubarak, being more interested in recognition and personal gain than in the preservation of human society, did not honor this agreement.

Q?

By all accounts, his bizarre behavior resembled the symptoms of certain neurological disorders—tics and spasms, bouts of catatonia, babbling—except that the progression of these symptoms was far too dramatic. He danced spasmodic jigs in lunch-hour traffic and once spent an entire day on the Piccadilly line of the London underground, ropes of drool hanging from his lips, traveling the loop around Heathrow over and over until early in the morning, when the conductor had him removed by police. Shortly after urinating on Ed Bradley during an interview for 60 Minutes, Mubarak went missing, and a few days later his body was fished from a gate on the Thames barrier, east of the city.

Q?

It's true that accident or suicide is the widely held view.

Q?

I am aware of the actual circumstances of his death, but I'll decline to divulge them, except to say that Ed Bradley had nothing to do with it.

Q?

By now I was near death myself. The others had been gone for a week when Mubarak's housekeeper, a girl named Lily Gabriel Holland, eased open the door to the spare room and peered in. Seeing us, she pushed the door open wide and entered the room, tall and bold, a Christian girl cursing her Muslim employer in his own home.

Q?

Initially she thought we were all dead. Tears spilled onto her cheeks, but her voice was strong and steady. "What has that bastard done?" she said, moving slowly from cage to cage.

I was too weak to rise. "Help me," I said.

Lily grasped the bars of my cage and shook them with sturdy hands. "You're alive," she said.

"I'm alive," I said. "Barely."

"How are you speaking to me?"

"Your God is dead," I told her.

"Yes," she said. She gave the cage another shake, and examined the padlock on the door. "There are rumors circulating in Mandela, though the government has tried to keep it quiet. People are more frightened of no-God than of the soldiers. So they are talking. They say Mubarak has something to do with this."

"I can explain," I said. "But for now—"

"Yes, no, of course!" she said, rising quickly to her feet. "I'll find something to open this cage." She left the room, returning a moment later with a hammer and pry bar. She wedged the sharp end of the bar against the latch, raised the hammer high above her head, and snapped the lock with one powerful stroke.

Q?

Lily was slender but very strong, and she carried my wasted body several miles through the streets to the slum of Mandela, where she shared a room with her father in a long dormitory-type building.

Q?

Like Lily, her father was kind, helping to care for me, fetching water from the neighborhood well, and grinding pigeon hearts into a paste I could digest. But unlike her, he was feeble, with spindly shriveled arms and a weakness for homemade liquor distilled from dates.

Q?

When I'd recovered my strength, I confirmed for them the reports they'd been hearing: The Creator was dead, and the first tremors of this revelation were being felt around the world. I told them, too, how I'd unwittingly eaten part of the Creator and been transformed.

"Then you are him," Lily's father said.

"What?" Lily said. "No, Papa."

"Isn't it clear?" her father said. "He ate God's body. Here he sits, a dog who talks like a person. He tells us things of a world we've never heard of. America! What does anyone here know of America, except its name? Yet he knows. He knows everything."

"I'm not your God," I said.

"He's not God, Papa," Lily told him.

"I know what I know," her father said, drinking from a jar of date liquor.

Q?

Lily guarded me closely, even from her father. Tension was gathering in the slum. People disappeared almost daily, taken by soldiers to Omdurman prison for blasphemy and incitement. Army trucks ground slowly over dirt streets, broadcasting orders for residents to attend churches and mosques on the appointed days of worship. Lily found this bitterly humorous.

"They must be desperate," she said. "Before, they bulldozed our churches and built apartment complexes on the rubble. Now they want us to show up every Sunday, without fail."

One night I pretended to sleep while Lily and her father argued about me.

"He could help people," her father said.

"It's too dangerous," Lily said, "if the government found out about him. And they would."

"He could give people hope. My friends—they want to know the future will be better."

"And what if it won't be, Papa?" Lily asked pointedly.

"Other things," he said, sidestepping her question. "What has happened to their families, for instance. Years of wondering, of suffering, could come to an end."

"Ah," Lily said, "now the truth comes out. We're not talking about your friends, are we, Papa? We're talking about you. What *you* want to know."

"Yes! Of course! And I hope you would be interested to know what became of your mother and sisters, too."

"I already know, Papa. They're dead."

After a few seconds of silence, he responded. "You think you know so much," he said, but his voice was quiet now, almost a whisper.

Q?

Lily was right; her mother and two older sisters were dead, killed by the goat farmer they'd been sold to after being kidnapped by the Janjaweed fifteen years earlier. But when her father came to me one afternoon while Lily was out bartering for wheat flour and lentils, I didn't have the heart to tell him their fate. He'd been kind to me, and I wanted to return that kindness.

Q?

I said they'd escaped the farmer and were living together in Darfur, near Nyala. I told him they were hoping still, after all the years, that he and Lily would return to them.

Now, in retrospect, I think of this as the moment when I truly joined the human pack.

Q?

Lily was angry, with her father for asking, and with me for giving an answer. She asked if it was true, if her mother and sisters were still alive. Not knowing what else to do, I told her that it was.

She cried all that night, while her father swore off date liquor and went about Mandela, relating my story and making plans to bring in people from the neighborhood to commune with me.

Q?

The next morning people began to arrive, bearing clothing, jewelry, sandalwood, crumpled wads of dinars, baskets of food. Lily's father collected the offerings and led people in one by one. Most, especially the women, immediately fell to their knees before me; others were more skeptical and did not genuflect until they heard my voice in their heads. Some were Christian, some were Muslim. They wanted to learn about the future, and the past. They asked after fathers who had disappeared, grandmothers long since dead, sons who had turned to thievery. When the honest answer was bad, which was most of the time, I lied to them. I told them that their dead fathers would return, that their grandmothers were happy in an afterlife I knew did not exist, that their psychotic sons would someday repay their love tenfold. I pretended to heal children who had only weeks to live, and called down great fortunes on the poorest of the poor. Every person I saw departed happy, their faces streaked with tears of shock and gratitude. Some even searched their pockets for anything else they could offer me, scattering coins and bits of lint on the dirt floor. By the time night fell, a growing crowd had clogged the street outside the room, and Lily's father told them to go home and return in the morning.

Q?

That night he cooked a feast of sorghum, corn, and lamb chops. Lily refused to eat; she sat silently on her cot, staring through the room's single window at the people still waiting in the street, their hopeful faces lit by flickering kerosene flames. After dinner her father counted up the offerings, and though his hands trembled for want of a drink, he smiled and waved the money in the air.

"Soon we'll have enough to travel to Nyala," he said to Lily. But she gave no sign that she heard him.

Q?

She watched in silence as word spread and people came to Mandela from as far away as Uganda and the Congo. They brought fear, despair, and money, and left that room relieved of all three. Many of these pilgrims brought their families and erected makeshift shelters. In two weeks the population of Mandela swelled by thirty thousand. At night they lit fires and sang songs of praise, united in their new devotion.

Q?

It did bother me, taking their meager belongings in exchange for lies, however well-intentioned those lies were. What bothered me more was Lily's disapproving stare. But I craved inclusion so desperately, and now I had it, or at least I thought I did. It didn't occur to me then that being an object of worship is possibly the greatest exclusion of all.

Q?

It ended as Lily had predicted—the government learned that people were making pilgrimages to Mandela, worshipping a dog as if he were God, and they sent troops in. The night they stormed the slum, rain fell hard, beating a violent rhythm on tin roofs, and while the people around me assumed the distant rumblings were thunder, I knew better.

"They're coming, Lily," I said. "Men in half-tracks, with rifles. They're coming for me."

"The people will fight them," she said. "They'll fight and die for you." It sounded like an accusation.

"I don't understand this," I said.

"You need to go," she said. "But before you do, I want to ask: Why did you lie to me about my mother and sisters?"

I didn't respond.

"Why?" she said again.

And for the first time in weeks, I spoke the truth. "I don't know," I told her.

Q?

Lily lifted me through the window, and I fled. I ran south through endless crowds of worshippers surging in the other direction, toward the fighting. In the darkness not one person noticed me, and I ran until the desert swallowed me again. I didn't stop until the sand became dry beneath my paws, until I had outrun the rains.

Q?

Hundreds of people died that night, including Lily. She was the only one among that crowd who fought for the right reasons. She stood tall in the rain and threw rocks. She used her strong hands to wrest a rifle from a soldier's grasp, and before she turned the gun on him she told him her mother's name, and made sure he heard it clearly.

Q?

Her father was taken prisoner and died a few months later at Omdurman, poisoned by a bad batch of cell-brewed liquor.

Q?

How do I feel about it? Let me answer you this way: I've

never returned to Khartoum, or any other place where people gather. I live as a normal dog, though hunting by myself is difficult and I'm often lonely. I haven't spoken to a person since that night, until now. That's how I feel about it.

Q.

No, that isn't the end. There's one other question you've neglected to ask. The question you came halfway around the world to have answered.

Q?

Don't be coy. I know things, remember. I know, for instance, that you are no different from any of the thousands of supplicants I've met with, except in this regard: I've told you the truth. And so you shouldn't need to ask your question, because you already have the answer.

Q.

Correct. The answer is, I don't have an answer. I can offer no comfort and little insight. I am not your God. Or if I am, I'm no God you can seek out for deliverance or explanation. I'm the kind of God who would eat you without compunction if I were hungry. You're as naked and alone in this world as you were before finding me. And so now the question becomes: Can you abide by this knowledge? Or will it destroy you, empty you out, make you a husk among husks?

The Helmet of Salvation and the Sword of the Spirit

Cursed be he that doeth the work of the Lord deceitfully, and cursed be he that keepeth back his sword from blood.

—Jeremiah 48:10

EVO-PSYCHS TAKE NEW GUINEA

PoMo Forces Abandon "Untenable" Positions in Australia;
Withdraw to Hawaiian Islands

With the Postmodern Anthropologist 8th Fleet, the Pacific Ocean (AP)—Evolutionary Psychologist forces, spearheaded by the human wave tactics of the Chinese, seized the capital of Port Moresby on Wednesday, effectively eliminating the last organized Postmodern Anthropologist resistance on the island of New Guinea. Three thousand PoMo Marines, refusing to abandon the capital along with the bulk of the defenders, were taken prisoner and subsequently put to death.

"It is in our nature to destroy the weak," Evo-Psych Premier Nguyen Dung said in a statement. "Thus, we had no choice but to execute your soldiers. But we do apologize. In fact, we apologize for this entire war. Sadly, it is in our nature to fight. And we are helpless against our nature. As are you."

Parents just didn't understand.

Arnold found himself thinking this more and more often in the latter half of his sixteenth year. He was thinking it now, as he sat on his rock on his beach and watched the ferry recede into the horizon where blue met blue, pursued by seagulls which never seemed to figure out that it wasn't a fishing boat and there were no free meals to be had. He'd dropped the grim weight of his book bag on the ground, where the sand was still wet from high tide, and when he slung the bag over his shoulders for the walk home it would be damp against his back and stink of dead clams. But he didn't care. He lit a cigarette, trying and failing to appear practiced and nonchalant about it, like the leathery fishermen on the mainland who seemed to have half-smoked Pall Malls surgically implanted on their lips. He took shallow drags and inhaled carefully. He watched the ferry and felt contemplative and full of important thoughts. He was putting on a show for an imagined audience of one. And though he knew at any moment he could have a real and unwelcome audience, in the form of his mother Selia, he didn't care about this, either.

He was in love. And that, among other things (such as Arnold's growing faith in Postmodern Anthropology), was what his father and Selia didn't understand.

Arnold was smart enough to realize, though, that as different as life was now, some things had always been more or less the same. When his father and Selia were teenagers, they surely had had clashes with their folks over this sort of stuff. Well, maybe not his father. But Selia, definitely. Arnold could imagine her staying out past curfew, driving fast and loose, outdrinking rough boys she was forbidden to be with, then taking them to bed. Maybe falling in love with one of those rough boys. Having a big blowup over it with her father, and running away for a while. The only difference now was that she and his dad didn't disapprove of *who* Arnold loved—in fact, they had never met Amanda, and neither had Arnold, for that matter. Their issue was with *how* he loved her. And this was where they just didn't understand, because the world had changed but they hadn't changed with it.

This is how love was, now: Arnold sat and imagined he was being observed tenderly from an unapproachable distance by Amanda. She was everywhere and nowhere at once, watching him, as he sat here smoking on his beach, or whistling a tune in the shower, or listening to a lecture in class on the evils of Evolutionary Psychology. No matter where he went or what he did, Amanda was with him, and this sense of being observed, even as he slept, produced in Arnold a constant, consuming exhilaration from which there was no relief.

Not that he sought relief. In fact, he reveled in the excitement of love as only a teenager can, scrawling page after page of poetry in Amanda's honor, sending hundreds of messages to her phone every day (which she never replied to, thankfully, because to have real contact with her, to start an actual dialogue, would ruin everything, and this was understood intuitively by Arnold and all the kids he knew). He did not so much as brush his teeth without considering how he appeared to Amanda, whether or not she would approve of his posture, his choice of circular strokes as opposed to vertical, the way he scrunched his face up to reach the molars in the back.

He was preparing to flick away the spent butt of his cigarette in a casual move Amanda would find pleasing when Selia appeared at the top of the bluff, her pantlegs rolled up in wide cuffs, clam-digging gear in hand.

"Shit," Arnold said under his breath. He hurried to dispose of the cigarette and the flick became more of a drop; the butt followed a weak trajectory down and landed in the sand a few inches from his boot. Amanda would not be impressed.

"You've taken up smoking now?" Selia said as she approached him, her bare feet leaving behind prints that filled with seeping seawater. "Fuel to the fire, eh, kiddo?"

Arnold said nothing. When his mother was upset, it was best to just take his licks and wait for it to be over. She could talk circles around him, and any attempt to explain or argue would only increase the severity of the tongue-lashing.

Selia handed him the pail, with the rake and shovel inside. Still talking, she rolled her pantlegs up further until they were above her knees. "Don't sweat it. I don't care. After all, I'm just some old bat who happens to be your ma. Smoke if you want to. Smoke a pipe. Smoke some weed. Smoke ground banana peels." Finished with her pants, Selia held her hands out, and Arnold turned over the gear without a word. "Run off and join the army, while you're at it," Selia continued. "Go to the war. Get shot full of holes for the glory of PoMo Anthropology. Kill a whole platoon of Evo-Psychs with nothing but a soupspoon. See if I care."

Arnold ventured only a sullen stare in response. He knew Amanda would want him to speak up, defend himself, assert his independence. But when it came to Selia, he was prepared to defy her only indirectly—sneaking cigarettes, for example. Besides, even when she was just guessing, his mother always seemed to be right. He'd been reading the war news, how the Evolutionary Psychologist armies had taken New Guinea and most of Australia. And he'd been thinking, with a curious admixture of dread and eagerness, that as a member (even a junior one) of the PoMo Party, he was duty-bound to defend his faith, especially at so crucial a time.

Plus, the thought of cutting a heroic swath through the Evo-Psych lines in Amanda's sight made his groin tingle.

But how did his mother always know these things, even when they never left his head?

After a few moments when neither of them spoke, Selia's eyes softened a bit, and she held the shovel out to him. "Hey," she said. "Help me find the clam shows."

Arnold hesitated. Just because he was afraid to fight openly with Selia didn't mean he had to accept a truce. He hadn't dug clams with her for a long time, though when he was younger, before he started attending school on the mainland, they'd gone digging together nearly every day. It was something he'd enjoyed, being united in purpose with his mother, being useful as something more than an object of adoration, carrying the great bucket of clams home by himself, with both hands. His father would already have a kettle on the gas stove, steam shooting from under the lid. And the eating of food he'd earned by his own work—fingers wet with butter and sea salt, the laughter around the table—had been a deep satisfaction to Arnold, even as a child.

But he was not a child anymore. And these days dinner was, more often than not, a silent, joyless affair. He refused the shovel Selia offered by turning away and lifting his book bag from the sand.

Selia shrugged. "Suit yourself," she said. Her tone struck Arnold as a bit too indifferent, and he winced to realize he'd wounded her, though that was exactly what he'd intended.

■

In his bedroom Arnold lit the two candles on the shelf beneath the framed photo of Amanda that hung on the wall. He sat on his bed and checked his cell phone, that essential apparatus of teenage society which his father had recently agreed to buy for him despite Selia's protests. There were 253 new text messages, all of them from Lisa Beard, a sophomore at the girls' school on the mainland. This is how love was now—Arnold had his own supplicant (as did many kids his age) whom he did not know and to whose messages he never responded. He erased them without reading and typed in his own message, to Amanda:

119

Divine Amanda—open my lips, and my mouth will proclaim your praise.

Always,

Arnold sent the message. He put the phone down on the bed beside him, slid back against the headboard with his booted feet on the comforter, and thought a moment. He picked up the phone again and typed:

Divine Amanda—things are not good, and I need your help. I feel like I don't belong here anymore. There are bigger things that I'm bound for, things I know you would want me to do. PoMo Anthropology teaches us that what we do in life, the kind of people we become, is up to us. But I don't know if I'm ready.

Always,

Arnold sent the message, then groped around in the book bag for his copy of the *Institutional Selves* textbook. He flipped to the section that Mr. Oswalt had assigned them to read, but couldn't manage more than a few paragraphs at a time before his attention wandered and his thoughts drifted to Amanda. He sent her another brief, pious message and tried again to read, but almost of their own accord his eyes moved to the framed picture of Amanda, mounted on the wall opposite his bed for easy viewing. The photo was a blown-up copy from the girls' school yearbook. Amanda's eyes, bisected by a loosely curled lock of blond hair that fell across her forehead, flickered in the light from the candles, the same blue as the ocean on Arnold's beach. Like the ocean, her eyes stared into him, steady and benevolent. Arnold felt that exquisite thrill rising slowly, still new enough to make him breathless, until he had no choice but to relieve it in the only way he knew how. Which he did, and quickly, to avoid being caught. He cleaned himself up with a handful of tissues, then deposited these in the bottom of the trash can under his desk. After sending one more message to Amanda, he turned back to the textbook and managed to read twenty pages before his father knocked twice, quietly.

"Come in," Arnold said.

His father opened the door. "Dinner," he said.

Arnold did not look up from his book. "Okay. I'll be right there."

His father remained in the doorway. "Arnie," he said, "you know it drives your mother nuts when you put your shoes on the bed."

Still reading, Arnold swung his feet until they hung awkwardly off the side.

"Nice effort," his father said. "But my point is, you don't *have* to do things just because they upset her."

At this Arnold looked up. "Dad," he said, "I'm a postmodern anthropologist. I don't *have* to do anything. I choose my own fate."

"Okay," his father said, trying to suppress an indulgent smile. "But so you know your fate is going to be a painful death at your mother's hands if she catches you with your shoes on the bed again."

PACIFIC THEATRE SITUATION "DESPERATE"

PoMo Marines in Kauai, Oahu Prepare "Alamo" Defenses

With the 3rd Postmodern Anthropologist Marine Expeditionary Brigade, Kauai (AP)—Marines on this westernmost island in the Hawaiian archipelago continued to prepare Wednesday for an attack by Evo-Psych forces, laying tank traps, erecting pillboxes on hills overlooking the beaches, and fortifying artillery emplacements. Meanwhile, units retreating by ship from the defeat at New Guinea began to arrive late Tuesday. "Nothing is inevitable, of course," said Colonel Francisco Garcia, commander of the 3rd Marine Expeditionary Brigade. "There are many perspectives from which to consider the situation, as we know. But it seems fairly certain that an assault will come in the next few weeks. And we are at a grave disadvantage in manpower, even with the units arriving from Australia and New Guinea."

■

"One of our great dilemmas," Mr. Oswalt said to the class, "raised by the text you were assigned to read, is how to strike a balance between our principles, as Postmodern Anthropologists, and our security—or, put more dramatically, the survival of our way of life. Does anyone have any thoughts on this?"

Most of the boys were preoccupied with the sight of a bull moose grazing in the baseball field outside the window. Arnold, seated toward the rear of the classroom, wondered if Amanda would want him to raise his hand.

"Mr. McCutcheon?" Oswalt said, striding slowly between the rows of desks.

Kelly McCutcheon cleared his throat. "I don't really understand the question."

Oswalt pushed up his glasses with one finger. "Did you do the reading?"

"Most of it."

"Most of it," Oswalt repeated. "Translation: You skimmed a few pages." He returned to the front of the classroom and leaned against his own desk. "Anybody have an idea what I'm driving at here?" he asked.

Arnold said, "We believe that no one paradigm is superior to another."

"Riiight," Oswalt said. "It's there in the Constitution for everyone to read: *Congress shall make no law regarding epistemologies, as different theories offer different perspectives and are therefore equally valid.* And so . . ."

Arnold hesitated. "I'm not really sure how to put it."

"You could put it quite simply," Oswalt said, "and say that our war with the Evolutionary Psychologists violates the very principles we're fighting to defend. After all, Evo-Psych is just another of the paradigms protected by our Constitution."

At this, an angry chorus went up among the twenty boys in the class.

"Yeah, but they're evil!"

"They started the war!"

"Evo-Psychs are savages! All they understand is violence!"

Oswalt raised his hands in a shushing gesture. "Before you get too excited, gentlemen, understand that I'm agreeing with you. They *did* start the war. They *are* savages. This is precisely the reason that, even in societies as advanced and enlightened as ours, principles must sometimes be sacrificed in order to meet and overcome threats."

Mike Raboteau, who had been staring silently at his desktop the entire period, spoke without looking up. "I hate them," he said.

Oswalt went to Mike and put a hand on his shoulder. "And with good reason, Mr. Raboteau. With good reason."

Outside on the baseball field, the moose raised its head, displaying a rack six feet across with too many points to count. It moved toward the home dugout, its long, multijointed legs unfurling languidly.

"That will do it for today," Oswalt said. The boys rose from their desks and gathered their books and cell phones. "We'll be discussing chapters twenty-six through thirty next week, so please be sure you've read them. And I'll expect to see you at the parade on Sunday to honor Mr. Raboteau's brother Paul. Enjoy your weekend."

■

Arnold smoked on the ferry home to ensure that there was no way Selia could catch him. He spent the afternoon helping his father in the garden. Together they weeded the rows and picked cucumbers and carrots for a salad, which Arnold prepared while his father broiled fillets of striped bass.

At dinner Arnold kept his phone on the table near his plate, putting down his fork every few minutes to type a message to Amanda.

"Does he ever actually *talk* on that thing?" Selia asked.

"It's mostly text," Arnold's father said. "That's how the kids use them these days."

Divine Amanda, Arnold typed. *I am a coward.*

"Yeah, well, the kids are doing a lot of things these days that don't make much sense," Selia said. "How do they even plan to *mate,* for Christ's sake?"

"It's a developmental phase, Selia. Studies show they graduate from it and have normal relationships."

"You're the expert. But perhaps he could take a break from developing long enough to have a meal with us."

How can I find the courage to go to war, Arnold typed, *when I can't even stand up to my mother?*

"I wish he'd put it away during dinner," Selia said. "It's rude."

"So is talking about someone as if they're not here in the room with you," Arnold's father said.

"Stick up for him, like always."

His father sighed. "Arnie, put the phone away."

I'm too much like my father. Content with keeping the peace, Arnold typed. *You must be ashamed of me. But I will do better.*

Always,

Arnold sent the message and put the phone in his hip pocket. "There's a parade on Sunday," he said, flaking his bass with the fork. "For Mike Raboteau's brother."

"The boy who was killed in New Guinea?" his father asked.

"Yeah."

"Ghastly war," Selia said.

"I'll go with you, if you like," Arnold's father said.

"And I'll stay here," Selia said, "and ponder the reasons why we moved to this island in the first place."

"You do that, Selia," Arnold said, before he could clamp his mouth shut over the words.

A shocked silence hung in the air over the table. Arnold's father closed his eyes and rubbed at them with the thumb and forefinger of one hand.

"Okay, Arnold, let's have it," Selia said. "Boy, has this been a long time coming."

"I don't want to fight, Ma," Arnold said.

"No, of course you don't. You'd rather defy me quietly, and sulk around as if I live for the pleasure of making your life miserable. Well, now the gauntlet's down. What do you have to say? Let's hear it."

"Nothing. Look, I'm sorry, Ma."

"Changed your mind? Okay. But I have a few things I'd like to get off my chest, if that's all right with you."

"Selia . . ." Arnold's father began.

"No. He needs to hear this. Besides, if you didn't indulge him so much we wouldn't be having this conversation. *You* decided it was okay for him to go to that propaganda factory they call a school—"

"He needed to be around kids his age," Arnold's father said.

"*You* bought him the phone. So maybe you could try being part of the solution, for once."

Arnold's father tossed his napkin on his plate, folded his arms across his chest, said nothing.

Selia turned her attention back to Arnold. "I think you need a little perspective. Here's the thing—you've only ever known one world, the one you were born into. But your father and I have been around long enough to see three very different worlds, and each new one has been worse than the last. So that by the time this Postmodern Anthropology nonsense started, *we*"—here she looked pointedly at Arnold's father—"*we* decided that we wanted nothing more to do with it."

But I'm not you, Arnold thought and did not say.

"I mean, come on, kiddo. Don't you think sometimes I'd like to have neighbors? A manicure? Electricity? But the trade-off— having to live among those PoMo psychos, to watch them send their kids off to the slaughter—isn't worth it."

Arnold looked down at his fish, studied the greasy flap of skin where he'd eaten the meat away.

"You think I'm a big-time bitch," Selia said. "I can live with that. Comes with the territory, really—you're sixteen, so by default I'm an old fucker who just doesn't get it. Fine. All I ask is that you consider the possibility that the reason I'm hard on you is not because I enjoy it, but because contrary to popular opinion, you're still a few years removed from knowing everything about everything."

Arnold pushed his plate away, a tiny gesture.

"Also, because I love you," Selia said.

"May I be excused?" Arnold asked.

"Arnie, we need to sit here and hash this out," his father said, but Selia waved her hand and Arnold was gone, up the stairs to his bedroom, fishing the phone from his pocket as the door swung shut behind him.

Divine Amanda, he typed. *For the first time, I feel sorry for my mother. I don't think she's ever believed in anything her whole life.*

SUICIDE ATTACKS IN MELBOURNE

PoMo Partisans Detonate Bombs in Stadium, Harbor

Evolutionary Psychologist–occupied Melbourne (AP)— PoMo resistance forces staged a series of coordinated suicide bombings here Saturday, killing an estimated 75 Evo-Psych shock troops and destroying a staging area where soldiers boarded transport ships in preparation for the impending assault on Hawaii. As many as a dozen civilians were also killed in the blasts.

"While we regret the loss of our soldiers, and the slight delay to our plans for invading Hawaii," Evo-Psych Premier Nguyen Dung said in a statement, "we applaud your insurgents for obeying their nature and continuing to fight."

∎

Sunday was warm for mid-April, with plenty of sunshine, a postcard day ideal for a parade. Arnold and his father took the ferry to the mainland, then followed the crowds downtown, where people were lined up ten and twelve deep along the concourse, waiting for the procession to begin and jockeying for the best views. Young children drifted above the crowd on their fathers' shoulders, clutching miniature flags in tiny fists. Without having to be asked, people made room on the roadside for the old and disabled to sit in lawn chairs.

The parade started promptly at ten. From where they were standing, on the western edge of the concourse, Arnold could hear things before he saw them. First he heard the slow approach of a song blaring from loudspeakers. As it drew closer he recognized the tune as "Proud to Be a PoMo," a country hymn that had been wildly popular during the last war, when Arnold was still being homeschooled. Now, though, the song had been set to a driving dance beat, and a group of girls, ranging in age from six to ten and dressed in spangled purple leotards and tap shoes, was dancing a poorly synchronized routine to the thump of the bass. Behind them followed an armored personnel carrier, two artillery pieces towed by camouflaged trucks, and a tractor trailer with a picture silk-screened on its side of grim but handsome young men in uniform. "The Few. The Proud," it read.

The crowd applauded as the parade rolled slowly past them for more than twenty minutes. Fire engines flashed their lights and sounded air horns. Marching bands marched, as did a small and hobbled group of veterans in old uniforms that were now a poor fit. Shriners provided comic relief, racing figure eights in undersized cars, their knees jammed up around their ears. The last vehicle in the procession, a convertible, held Mike Raboteau and his parents, who gave weak, perfunctory waves to the cheering crowd.

A portable stage had been erected in the center of the concourse, beneath the shade of the town's Free Will tree, a stately old elm which had been transplanted to the spot when the original Free Will tree, dedicated as a sapling, had fallen victim to beavers. The convertible lurched to a halt when it reached the tree, and the town mayor and a tall, grizzled man wearing a Marine uniform greeted the Raboteaus as they mounted the stairs leading up to the stage.

After the family had been seated the mayor approached the podium at center stage and spoke into the microphone. "Thank you all for coming today," he said, his amplified voice echoing off the brick facades of the buildings that surrounded the concourse. "Your presence does honor to our fallen hero, Corporal Paul Raboteau, and his family. Many of us knew Paul as a smart, honest young man and a dedicated member of the Postmodern Anthropologist Party. Having known him has brightened and enriched our lives, and having lost him, especially at a time when we need all the Paul Raboteaus we can find, grieves us beyond words."

The crowd, so energized only a few minutes before, now grew quiet and still under the mayor's eulogy.

"As many of you know, Paul was one of the Marines who refused to retreat from New Guinea, choosing to face almost certain death rather than yield another inch of ground to the Evolutionary Psychologists. He died in a distant, foreign land, separated from those he loved, but no doubt comforted by his faith in Postmodern Anthropology and the righteousness of our struggle. All of us, I'm certain, are humbled by this act of courage and selflessness. While it's clear that nothing we do will compare to the sacrifice that Paul has made on the altar of free will, still we must do what we can to celebrate and memorialize that sacrifice, and to encourage others to follow his example. To that end, I declare that today's date, April sixteenth, will henceforth be celebrated in this city as Corporal Paul Raboteau Day, so that we may be reminded of this brave young man, and so that his name and his story will not be forgotten by future generations."

The people assembled burst into delirious applause. Flags waved. A boy of two or so standing near Arnold began to bawl soundlessly, his cries drowned out by the uproar.

The mayor raised his hands for quiet. "Thank you. Thank you. Please. The Colonel has something to add. Ladies and gentlemen, Colonel Gene Redmond."

The uniformed man stepped to the podium amidst another burst of applause. He ran one hand over the bristles of his salt-and-pepper hair. "I doubt anyone could follow that," he said, casting a smile over his shoulder at the mayor, who had taken a seat. "So I won't try. I just wanted to announce that young Michael Raboteau here has recognized the military's need for every able-bodied young man we can get, and decided to forgo his final year of high school to join the Marines. His parents, despite the loss they've already endured, have given their blessing for him to do so. Not that they had a choice in the matter, mind you, but that's not the point. Folks, these people are truly pillars of the community. You should be stopping them on the street to thank them at every opportunity. You should be giving them free oil changes and satellite television service. You should be showing up at their door to do their shopping and walk their dog. Better yet, you should be following their lead and making sacrifices of your own. Thank you."

Further applause from the crowd, slightly more subdued this time, but still powerful and sustained. Arnold's initial shock at the Colonel's announcement was already giving way to a deep, burning jealousy. He clapped along absently, standing on the tips of his toes to catch a glimpse of Mike Raboteau. But his view was mostly obscured by the podium, and all he saw was Mike's hand, clasped in the Colonel's larger one, pumping up and down in a warm, prolonged handshake.

EVO-PSYCH FLEET SHELLS HAWAIIAN DEFENSES

Invasion Considered "Imminent"

With the 3rd Postmodern Anthropologist Marine Expeditionary Brigade, Kauai (AP)—Shells from Evolutionary Psychologist ships fell on Marine positions here in the early-morning hours on Sunday. By the Marines' own estimate, 30 percent of the defensive structures on the immediate coastline, including concrete pillboxes, antiaircraft batteries, and artillery emplacements, were destroyed or rendered useless. In addition, daybreak revealed that tank traps and other defensive obstacles placed on the beach had been cleared with explosives by teams of Evo-Psych commandos.

•

Entering Mr. Oswalt's classroom on Monday, Arnold smelled Colonel Redmond before he saw him. Even with a window open the air in the room was laden with an unmistakably masculine scent, like Armor All mingled with cigar smoke. The Colonel sat on a stool in the corner, almost behind the door; Arnold moved to his place near the back of the room (past Mike Raboteau's desk, conspicuously vacant), wondering where the smell was coming from, and only noticed the Colonel when he turned to take a seat himself.

"Gentlemen," Mr. Oswalt said when everyone was seated, "I've got good news for those of you who neglected your reading this weekend—you've got another day to get it done. You'll remember Colonel Redmond, whom many of you saw at the parade yesterday—except of course for Messieurs Davis and McCutcheon, whom I'll have words with after class. The Colonel has asked that he be allowed to speak with you, and I agreed to give him today's period to discuss the military's need for new recruits and, as well, the obligation that you bear to defend Postmodern Anthropology. Colonel?"

"I don't know about all that," the Colonel said, rising from the stool and smoothing the front of his uniform. He grinned, revealing teeth too square and white to belong to a man his age. "Not to undercut your teacher here, boys, but I bet if I started going on and on about free will versus genetic predetermination and how PoMo Anthro is superior to Evolutionary Psychology in every which way—well, I bet your eyes would just gloss over and you'd drift off on some daydream until this old soldier finished with his spiel and left you alone. I mean, you get that sort of thing in here every day, and man, you're sick of it. Am I right?"

The grin widened, inviting them to admit they had little interest in yet another ideological sermon. Most of the boys, except for Arnold and Kelly McCutcheon, cast nervous glances in the direction of Mr. Oswalt, then slowly ventured smiles of their own.

"So what I'd like to talk about instead—well, it's two things. First thing I want to talk about is guns. You boys like guns, right?"

An affirmative murmur rippled through the classroom.

"Well, let me tell you, when it comes to guns nobody can hold a candle to the PoMo Marines." The Colonel ran a hand over his stubbled scalp in the same gesture Arnold had noticed the day before. "Now some of you have probably gone hunting with a 12-gauge or some pussy-ass .22. You may even have an old man who's a gun nut and had a few beers one day and said to himself, *Self, the boy's growing up quick. Probably time to let him try the old .45 on for size.* But I'd be willing to wager my retirement—and it's pretty substantial, boys—that you've never even laid eyes on a CAR-15 assault rifle with a bottom-mounted M203 grenade launcher, much less fired one. If any of you have, tell me and I'll cut you a check from my pension right this minute."

Silence from the group.

"That's what I thought," the Colonel said. "How about an M134 minigun? We're talking a rate of fire near six thousand rounds per minute. Just one round can crack the engine block on a semi. No shit. Or how about the AT4 anti-armor rocket? Turn an Evo-Psych tank into a flaming hunk of junk with one little twitch of the trigger. Have any of you ever felt the kick from one of those babies? Sound off loud and clear so I can hear you."

"No," the boys said in one voice.

"No, *sir*," the Colonel said.

"No, sir!"

"Well you will," the Colonel said, his voice suddenly low and conspiratorial. "If you join the Marines."

He turned away, taking a few steps back toward Mr. Oswalt's desk to let his words sink in.

"The other thing I want to talk about," he said after a moment, turning on one heel to face them again, "is money. Now, you've got a nice little town here. I noticed some decent places on the waterfront on my way in yesterday. But let's be honest— no one here is getting rich catching alewife and flounder, and that's what you boys are looking at when you leave this school— a lifetime of popping Dramamine and stinking like fish shit, and when you finally kick you'll be lucky to have enough cabbage to pay for your own casket. Any of you looking forward to that? Sound off, now."

"No, sir."

"Besides, what little money there is in this town doesn't belong to any of you," the Colonel said. "You want something, you've got to ask your old man to buy it for you. And that in my opinion is a shit state of affairs, for grown men like you not to be able to get what they want when they want it."

The Colonel leaned against Mr. Oswalt's desk. His voice dropped again into the conspiratorial hush. "So listen here," he said. "What if I told you that the Marines will give you twenty thousand dollars just for signing up? I wouldn't lie to you, boys. You show up at the recruitment center, sign a few forms, get a few shots, turn your head and cough, whammo—they cut you a check for twenty grand right there. Take it to the bank and cash it that afternoon. Now I want you to think about that a minute."

The Colonel folded his arms and gazed at the class, still smiling.

"You thinking about what you could buy with all that money?"

"Yes, sir!"

"Good. Take your time. There's lots of things a man should want."

Arnold, incredulous at the Colonel's performance, watched the red second hand wind slowly around the face of the clock on the wall behind Mr. Oswalt's desk.

"Okay," the Colonel said brightly, clapping his hands together. "That's it, boys. I don't need to sell this anymore, and you know it, because this shit sells itself. I assume you know where the recruitment center is here in town. Open seven days a week. Thanks for humoring an old man."

The boys looked to Mr. Oswalt, who nodded, and they rose and began filing out of the room. The Colonel stood at the front of the class, laughing and clapping backs, but when Arnold tried to slip through the doorway the Colonel put a hand on his shoulder and squeezed with surprising strength.

"Son," he said, "I noticed you weren't sounding off with the rest of the boys."

"No."

"No, *sir*."

"No, sir."

"Did you not like what I had to say?"

"No, sir, it's not that. I—"

"Son, I think I have an inkling what the problem is," the Colonel said. "You're a smart kid. That old guns-and-money routine won't work on you. But you're exactly the kind of young man I'm trying to reach. I'd trade in all the boys in this class for just one of you. And you know why?"

"No, sir."

"Because you know why we're really in this fight, and you care about it," the Colonel said. "So do I. What you saw here today, that's just a little recruiting razzle-dazzle. A sales pitch. I don't feel good about it. Never have. But we need warm bodies on the field, now more than ever. And this is the way to make that happen. Do you understand?"

"I think so, sir."

"More than that, we need men like you, son."

"Like me, sir?"

"Men with conviction," the Colonel said. "Men with heads on their shoulders. Men who can lead the guns-and-money bunch."

The Colonel unfastened the top button of his jacket, reached in, and removed a business card. "Take this for me," he said. "You think about it, and you give me a call. We'll talk."

"Sir, I don't—"

"Take the card, son. In a few days you'll be glad you have it."

■

Selia and Arnold hadn't spoken more than a few words to each other since the argument, but on Tuesday morning she stopped him on his way out to school and offered a bagged lunch of smoked Atlantic salmon, Brie, stone wheat crackers, and homemade pudding. Arnold knew his mother well enough to realize this was not a peace offering or an apology so much as an attempt to resume the discussion in a more civilized tone.

"Thanks," he said, taking the bag.

"Listen," she said. "Let's you and me take our dinner up to the natural pool tonight."

"Okay," he said. "What about Dad?"

"He's a big kid. He can feed himself."

The natural pool was a large bowl-shaped formation of granite on the north coast of the island that filled with seawater and small fish at high tide. As the sun retreated toward the mainland later that day, Arnold and Selia picked their way along the rocky shore leading to the pool, iridescent shards of clamshells snapping and gritting underfoot. They cast long early-evening shadows on skittish Jonah crabs and knots of seaweed that waved and shimmered in the unsettled water. On a flat slab of granite overlooking the pool, they spread a blanket and set out their dinner from the basket Selia carried.

Arnold knew his mother wanted to talk, but he offered no openings, giving curt one-word answers to her questions about school and gazing for long minutes out toward the horizon, where the delineation between sky and sea was fading along with the daylight. By the time they finished eating Selia had given up trying to spark a conversation. She lit a cigarette, the second of the two she allowed herself each day, and joined her son in watching the whitecaps roll in from the open ocean.

Arnold took his phone out and typed a message:

Divine Amanda: I've been noticing lately how I share many odd mannerisms with my father. The way I say hi to strangers on the street in a bright, clipped way, somehow shortening the word to half a syllable. Or how sometimes I catch myself pursing my lips when concentrating on a task, like setting the first few threads on a screw, just like he does. These behaviors could be learned, I guess, but the lip-pursing thing in particular seems for some reason to clearly be genetic.

Always,

Selia pushed her sunglasses back on her head and looked

over at him. "I wish you had half as much to say to me," she said, smoke drifting from her mouth as she spoke. "Hours and hours, typing away. What *do* you write about to that girl?"

Arnold didn't answer. Instead he began another message:

Divine, exquisite Amanda: Until yesterday I was certain it was time for me to leave here and join the Marines. After Colonel Redmond visited our class yesterday, though, I don't know what to think. All that idiotic crap about guns. Although he did pull me aside at the end and explain, told me that I was the kind of guy they were really looking for. Which may have been just another sales pitch, to use his term. I guess ultimately it doesn't matter whether he's sincere or not, whether or not he believes. What matters is whether or not I believe. And I do. I believe more in this than in anything else, except y—

"I asked you a question," Selia said, snatching the phone from Arnold before he could finish the message. She stood quickly and turned away from him, giggling as he got to his feet and tried to reach around her to take the phone back.

"How the hell do you work this thing?" she said.

"Mom," Arnold said. "Mom, give it back."

"I want to see what the big deal is," she said, turning to block his reach. "*Scroll up/down.* Okay, now we're getting somewhere."

"Mom!" Arnold said.

"Oh!" Selia's eyes went wide with amusement. *"Divine Amanda,"* she breathed, pressing the back of one hand to her forehead in a mock swoon. "Oh, this is rich, kiddo. This is really rich."

"Selia!" Arnold yelled. He'd stopped trying to take the phone from her and stood with his fists clenched at his sides. "Give me the fucking phone!"

But suddenly Selia wasn't laughing anymore, and she seemed not to hear him. The hand dropped from her forehead as she continued reading, scrolling down, reading. Arnold waited, breathing hard. His face burned with equal parts anger and shame. When Selia was finished she held the phone out to him, and he unclenched his fist and took it.

Without a word Selia set about gathering the plates and utensils and leftover food from their dinner, throwing them haphazardly into the basket. She picked up the blanket, wound it into a ball, and tossed it on top of the other things. Then she lifted the basket above her head and heaved it into the natural pool, where it landed with a splash, bobbed a moment on the ripples it had created, then slowly began to sink.

Selia watched the basket going down. "Here's something you don't know," she said, her voice barely audible over the pulse of the surf. "Years ago, your father had another son. Your half-brother. He died. So did your father's first wife. In one of those earlier worlds I was telling you about."

Arnold had no idea how to respond. A peculiar sensation of minute trauma had started up between his eyes, as though he were being tapped there repeatedly with a ball-peen hammer. He realized in a distant way that this was his heartbeat.

Selia turned to face him. "I hate you for making me say this," she said, and at the word *hate* Arnold felt suddenly much smaller than he was, impossibly small, like the infant he had no memory of being. Tears stung his eyes in an instant. "I hate you for making me sound like some hysterical idiot. But I have never been so sad or angry in my life, and all that's coming to mind right now are clichés. So here goes: If you join the Marines—if you go to that ridiculous war and break your father's heart again—you are not my son."

Selia's eyes were dry. She turned away from Arnold and retraced their path along the rocks, not looking back. Arnold watched her recede and felt the first sob rising from his gut to the back of his throat like a surge of vomit, and though he resisted, knowing Amanda would be ashamed of him, in a moment he was overcome. He sat on the edge of the granite slab with his legs dangling above the pool and typed through his tears:

ivine, amanda: fuck her fuck her fuck her fuck her fuck her

LOCAL BOY EARNS MARINE COMMISSION

By Linda Merrill, Staff Writer

Quantico, Virginia—Arnold Ankosky, 17, of Bar Harbor, completed OCS training at the Postmodern Anthropologist Marine Corps Officer Candidate School in Quantico on Thursday, part of a graduating class of 42. Ankosky was commissioned a 2nd Lieutenant and will be assigned to the 7th Marine Expeditionary Brigade, based in San Diego. The 7th is currently engaged in bitter fighting against Evolutionary Psychologist forces in Mexico's Sierra Madre mountains, where Ankosky will join them as a platoon leader.

My Brother the Murderer

And Cain said unto the Lord, My punishment is greater than I can bear.

—Genesis 4:13

Coming home from work on a Wednesday evening, I see an ocean of emergency vehicles massed outside the High Hopes Mental Health Center—ambulances and police cruisers, their lights painting the autumn night with bright flashes of red and blue. There are twenty or thirty of them, parked haphazardly along the road and in the center's parking lot. Some of the police cruisers are staties, and this is the first indication that something very bad has happened. The town I live in is small but has a sizable police force; the state troopers are called on only rarely, when the local police are in over their heads.

As a traffic cop waves me past with his hooded flashlight, I notice that parked among the ambulances and cruisers are three CNN news vans with out-of-state license plates, along with the local media.

I hurry home. The streets are empty and I run a red light. I don't bother stopping at the store for cigarettes and orange juice, as I had intended.

When I step through the front door I can hear the news on the television in the living room. Melissa is waiting for me. She is sitting at the kitchen table with her hands wrapped around a mug of tea. Her hair is pulled back in a loose ponytail and she has been crying. She gives me a strange look—sadness mostly, but something else too—revulsion, maybe? Or dread? I can't tell, but it's not good.

What is it, Lissa? I ask, though somehow I already know, somehow I knew the moment I saw all those police cars. What the hell's going on?

And she tries to tell me, but it takes her a while, because she keeps breaking into fresh tears and stopping short to collect herself and wipe her eyes. Once she stops in midsentence and stares down into her mug for several minutes without speaking. Eventually, though, she gets it all out, and I have to look down at my legs to make sure they're still there and I sit down with her at the table because otherwise I might collapse on the kitchen floor. The two of us sit silently for a while. Melissa sips her tea. I feel something warm slide down my face and drop from my chin and I look down and see a small circle of moisture on the table and realize that I'm crying now, too.

The newscast drones on in the background.

Some time later I reach for Melissa's hand, but she pulls it away. I look up at her and now there's no mistaking the expression on her face—it's fear.

■

The next day I call in sick to work. Soon I wish I hadn't, because the phone is ringing off the hook. Reporters. Hundreds of them, from all over the country, some from as far away as England and Italy. They want to ask me questions about my brother. I thought I was numb beyond surprise or shock, but some of the questions they ask get my chest burning, make my forehead break out in stinging beads of sweat.

What did your brother have against the counselors at High Hopes? they ask me.

Nothing, I say.

We've learned your brother was being treated there on an outpatient basis, they say. Why would he suddenly turn on them?

I don't know, I say. He's got things wrong with him. He always has.

Was there some sort of significance, they ask, to the use of the Virgin Mary statuette as a murder weapon?

A sudden anger bubbles up, and I want to say, I doubt it. Probably the first thing he got his hands on, but I know this would not be true, and even though Melissa won't come near me and I've already gotten some sidelong glances and whispered comments from the neighbors and the people at Joseph's Deli this morning as I was buying the orange juice I meant to get last night, I say, very evenly, How in the world would I know?

And then, very, very gently, I hang up the phone. But the moment I put it down, it rings again.

Over the ringing, I hear Melissa turn on the water in the bathroom. This is the third time she's showered today.

■

My parents haven't left their house since the murders. It's been two weeks. My father hasn't emerged at all, but at first my mother was determined not to be judged guilty by association, and she went without a word right past the group of reporters and cameramen who'd camped out in their front yard. She went to the grocery store and the bank and her Thursday night cribbage group.

But people started saying things around town, and pretty soon those things made their way into the newspapers. By now the national media had packed up and gone home, but the murders were still big news locally, and the front page was littered with rumors and accusations—of theism, closed-door worship, *Christianity*. This my mother could not take. So she stopped going out, and now I am doing their shopping and running their errands for them.

Today I had their cable TV turned off and canceled their newspaper delivery, at my mother's request. The looks I get from people on the streets and in stores have changed now from naked curiosity to compassion. That poor boy, they say to each other. To have to grow up in that house. Imagine.

Mike, who has been a friend of mine since grade school, comes to my house one evening with a meat pie from his wife.

Mike, I say. Why are people telling these lies about my parents?

I don't know, he says, shaking his head. They're just trying to make sense of this, you know? Find some sort of reason for all of it. They can't believe your brother could be so . . . they don't see how he could do something that . . . well, you know. Unless something bad had happened to *him*.

This is something else, now, that I've noticed—the few people I've talked to are very careful in choosing their words, as though they are afraid to say the wrong thing to me. What they don't seem to understand is there is no right thing to say.

I wish Mike wouldn't do this along with everyone else. We've been friends long enough, he can just say whatever comes to mind. But he won't.

Mike, I say. You know how my brother is. How he's always been.

Yeah, Mike says, and he's shaking his head again. But, I mean, why? Where did he get these ideas about a god? He must have learned them somewhere, right?

I take the pie and set it on the kitchen counter and thank Mike. I tell him to thank his wife. I almost add, Give her a hug for me. But then I think better of it.

■

I'm trying to be patient with Melissa. I've given her space. I sleep on the sofa. During the day I spend a lot of time outside in the yard, even though it's getting colder and autumn is passing into winter.

We haven't made love for a month. Once, a few days ago, the two of us were talking and drinking tea and something I said made her smile. It was a good moment, so I ventured a light kiss on her lips. But when I pulled back I saw goose bumps on her arms, and all the blood had drained from her face. I haven't touched her at all since then.

She has nightmares. I hardly sleep at all, so I lie awake on the sofa and listen to her moan and whimper. I want to go to the bedroom, wake her by smoothing her hair and speaking gentle, reassuring words. I want to bring her back to the real world and see the relief on her face when she opens her eyes and realizes it was just a bad dream. I cannot do any of this.

■

Even though I don't want to, I have to go back to work. My supervisor told me to take as much time as I needed (no one seems to know what the appropriate bereavement period is for this sort of thing), but the bills are piling up and Melissa's still not talking much, so I go to work.

My job is in quality control at the Chinet paper products factory. I punch in and go to my station and watch paper plates go by on the belt and remove the ones that have visible flaws. After four hours the whistle sounds and I go to lunch. Mike, who works in shipping and receiving, meets me in the cafeteria. The two of us sit at a table with Fred and Duke. I poke around in the bag lunch I packed for myself; Melissa didn't get out of bed to make my lunch as she used to. Mike and Fred and Duke talk about football. The Patriots are having another terrible season. Duke made the mistake of betting on them against the Packers last Sunday and lost fifty bucks. His wife is going to kill him, he says. If she finds out, he says. Then they mix in some talk about the war, the losses in the Pacific. It doesn't look good, they say. The three of them make an effort to include me in the conversation. They address questions directly to me. They want to know what I think about this and that, who looks to be the toughest team in the AFC, whether or not Trent Jackson will be able to hold the line in Mexico against the Evo-Psychs. But I haven't been keeping up with football this year, and the war seems as distant as Pluto, so I don't have much to say.

At one point, after I mumble something in reply to a question, the three of them are quiet for a moment, exchanging looks they think I don't notice.

After lunch my supervisor calls me into his office. He has me sit down and asks how things have been, if there's anything he can do. He is a good man. He came up from the factory floor himself, so he knows what it's like, and he cares about his workers.

My door's always open, he says, if you need to talk.

And suddenly my throat tightens up and my vision goes

blurry and I want to tell him everything: about Melissa and my parents and how I just want things to be the way they were before, but I clamp my teeth down over the words and say nothing, because control is paramount—I must maintain at least the appearance of normalcy if I ever want things to go back to normal.

Thanks, I say to him, and leave the office quickly before the tears spill out onto my cheeks.

■

Melissa's sister Lacy comes by a lot. The two of them sit at the kitchen table and talk and smoke cigarettes. Melissa drinks her tea. Lacy makes herself coffee with the jar of instant stuff we keep around. They keep their voices low. Even when I'm in the next room, I can't make out what they say.

One day while Lacy is visiting, I go outside in the red-and-black-checked wool jacket my grandfather gave me years ago, before he died. I put on a pair of work gloves and set about pulling up the remains of the small garden I and Melissa planted and tended this year. The corn, which was a bug-infested disappointment despite the extra attention I gave it, comes up easily. I pull the stalks and shake the loose dirt from the roots and throw them aside. Then I move on to the two big sprawling zucchini plants. These were a boon. It seemed like every day when I came home this summer there were two or three new zucchinis washed and drying on the kitchen counter. Big ones, too. All summer long Melissa made stuffed zucchini and zucchini bread and zucchini parmesan. The two of us ate dinner and joked about never wanting to see another zucchini as long as we lived. Still, the plants kept producing more at an amazing, impossible rate.

And now, even with their stalks knocked flat by frost and their leaves dead and wilted, the plants cling stubbornly to the soil. I dig around the roots with a hand spade and work the plants back and forth, trying to loosen their grip on the earth. I'm not making much progress. Then I hear the screen door slam and I look up and see Lacy standing on the porch. She has her jacket on and her car keys in her hand. She is looking at me.

Damn things don't want to die, I say to her as she comes down the steps and approaches me.

Why don't you just leave them? she asks.

It'll be a real mess in the spring, I say, if I don't pull them now.

I go back to digging, scooping dirt away with the hand spade. I feel strange with her just standing there, watching me dig, and neither of us saying anything.

Lacy is quiet for a moment longer. Then she says, You've got to do something. My sister needs you.

I look up. What am I supposed to do, Lacy? I ask.

She crosses her arms over her chest and says, I don't know. Something. She's coming apart, and you're out here gardening in the middle of November.

I get to my feet. She treats me like I'm a leper, I say. She needs help, sure. She may even want help. But she sure as hell doesn't want it from me.

I've drawn myself up to my full height, a good six inches taller than Lacy. She eyes the spade in my left hand. Then she looks up, into my eyes. I know what she's thinking. And even though I shouldn't, I speak in anger.

Go ahead, I say. Think whatever you want. Be afraid of me, like your sister is. But I'm not my brother. I haven't done anything.

Lacy takes a slow step backward, then another. She says, Maybe that's the problem. You haven't done anything.

Then she turns and goes to her car in the driveway.

I watch her get in and turn the ignition and back out. I glance at the house and think for a moment that I see Melissa's face behind the kitchen window: ghostly, watchful. But it's just a reflection in the glass.

■

My father eats very little. Some days he doesn't bathe, doesn't even bother gettting dressed, just shuffles around all day in his pajamas and bathrobe. Unlike my mother, he accepted what he thought was his part of the responsibility for what my brother did. That was before people started accusing them of worship.

If something is repeated often enough, with enough conviction, it doesn't seem to matter whether it's true. It becomes the truth. So mostly my father sits around in his pajamas and bathrobe and doesn't do much of anything. He might flip through a book or a magazine. He glances out the windows occasionally.

Some days he doesn't get out of bed.

My mother has started going out again, doing some light shopping, having her hair done. She went to her cribbage group one time, but says she won't anymore.

The trees are bare and my parents' yard is covered with a thick layer of leaves. The leaves were bright orange and red and yellow but have been lying around for a while and are all gradually becoming the same dark brown color, from rain and rot. A section of vinyl siding has come loose from the corner of their house and flaps back and forth in the November winds, slapping against the wall. A week ago someone tossed a rock through a window on the second floor and the pane hasn't been replaced. I patched the hole with a piece of particle board to keep the cold out, and no one, not me or my mother or my father, said a word about why someone might have done it. I prefer to think it was marauding kids, still jazzed up from Halloween and looking to cause trouble. So that's what I think.

■

One night Melissa is having her nightmares and the only sound in the house is her whimpering and crying and I do it—I get up off the sofa and go to her in the bedroom. I sit down carefully on the bed next to her. The room is dark except for silvery moonlight filtering in through the window but I can see some of her hair is clinging, tangled and thick with sweat, to her face, and I brush it away gently with just two fingers.

Lissa, I say to her, it's all right, baby. It's okay.

I say, It's me, Lissa. Nothing's changed, honey, it's just me, same as always.

Wake up now, I say. C'mon Lissa, wake up, baby.

She doesn't wake, but her crying stops and she nestles against my thigh in her sleep. I put a hand on her head. I watch the moon make its way slowly past the window. It's like watching the hour hand on a clock. I am very careful not to move.

■

My brother's trial lasts only four days. He is found not guilty by reason of insanity and sent to the state mental hospital in Augusta. Soon after, most people around town go on with their lives and forget about him and what he did. Every time they see me, though, their eyes flash, and they're reminded.

■

Winter comes. The first snow turns my parents' yard from brown to thick, pure white, and thankfully it stays. The flap of siding still hangs loose and the window on the second floor is still broken, but with the snow things don't look so bad.

My mother makes plans to go to Florida for the winter. She meets with a travel agent a few towns away and calls a realtor in Palm Beach. Every morning she pesters my father until he showers and puts on pants and shoes and a clean oxford. I don't have to do their shopping or run errands for them anymore; my mother does these things again. She goes from place to place with her head up and her back straight and stiff.

■

Melissa and me have been sharing our bed again for a while. One night she asks me to make love to her.

Are you sure? I ask.

I think so, she says. I need to try. I need to know.

I roll onto my side and face her. I put a hand on her bare shoulder and feel her start underneath my touch. I move on top of her and she kisses me, over and over, quick and desperate. She is trembling beneath me. When I move my hands to her face her cheeks are wet. She kisses me and her tears pour down warm over my knuckles.

Afterwards we lie apart on either side of the bed.

How could he have done that, Jim? Melissa says, and she is still crying a little. To those poor women?

■

My parents are gone. I helped them close up the house, and they left three days ago for a condo in Palm Beach.

Melissa is gone. She went up north, to her father's place in Presque Isle, where she will be snowed in and safe until April. She said she will be back sometime. It's not over, she said. I just need to get away for a while.

Tonight I drive to Augusta through a blizzard. The speed limit on the interstate has been dropped to 45 because of the weather. I can't see beyond the scrim of thick heavy snowflakes illuminated by my headlights, and it takes nearly an hour to cover the twenty miles there.

I am going to see my brother. There is something I need to do, to relieve me, and Melissa, and my parents, and my brother, of the burden his crime has become. For this I've brought my blackjack, another gift from my grandfather, an iron dowel wrapped like a sausage in scuffed leather. My grandfather used it to crack the heads of rowdy GIs when he was an MP in the army. Because it is deadly, the blackjack has been illegal for years, but I've kept it as a memento. And now I have a use for it.

There is something else I need from my brother, something I have to ask him, something I need to know. A few days ago, after my parents left and I went back to my empty house, I sat down on the sofa and put my head back and fell into a doze. Through the haze of sleep came something which felt like memory: I was a boy of six or seven, in an overgrown field behind the abandoned fire station near my childhood home. A friendly wrestling match with another boy, an older, stronger boy, had suddenly turned serious. I was pinned down; I could feel the sharp broken reeds of the straw grass pricking my back through my shirt. One hand held me down at the shoulder, another hit me repeatedly across the face, clumsily, flailing, but hard enough to draw blood from my lip. I squirmed and pushed but could not throw the older boy off of my chest, and so I cried, and even though this was the only thing left to me, the only thing the older boy could not keep me from doing, I still felt shame even through my fear.

And then my brother, who was much bigger and stronger than the older boy, appeared seemingly out of nowhere. He wound the fingers of one large hand into the boy's hair and lifted him. For a moment the boy hollered and squinted against the pain, reaching up blindly to grasp my brother's wrist, and then his cries were cut short by the impact of my brother's other hand, balled into a great fist, against his nose. Blood exploded from the boy's face like the bursting of a water balloon, and he went down, and my brother straddled his chest and now the older boy was the one crying and begging for mercy, while my brother spoke frightening words over and over in a voice I did not recognize, and even though my brother beat him badly enough to scare me and would not stop even when I screamed and pulled at his shirt there was a part of me, still is a part of me, that felt glad and proud to have a brother so big and strong and loyal, a brother I could count on.

But when I came to fully on the sofa, in the empty house, with Melissa gone, my parents gone, I couldn't tell whether this was just a dream or if it had really happened long ago. It bothered me, that I couldn't tell. As the days passed and the memory/

dream persisted, grew stronger and more vivid, it bothered me more, until I finally decided this afternoon to go see my brother and ask him if he remembers.

I pull cautiously off the interstate and follow the signs to the mental hospital. The streets are empty except for the big orange plow trucks, sweeping snow off to the side of the road and spitting sand in their wake. All the traffic lights are blinking yellow. I pass through them steadily, without touching the gas or the brake.

The hospital is set back maybe two hundred yards from the road. I pull off to the side and get out of the car and look down on the grounds. I'm surprised to see there are no walls, or fences topped with razor wire. From this distance the hospital could easily be mistaken for a small college campus. There are six or seven large brick buildings, well lit by orange floodlights. Most of the windows are dark; only a few, here and there, have lights on behind them. A pickup truck is plowing the long narrow driveway that leads down from the main road to the hospital proper.

I light a cigarette. The snow is coming harder now, driven by a gusting wind, and I have to squint to keep it out of my eyes. I smoke and look at the hospital and the river, black and frozen, behind it.

I remember the sun, hot and fat over the field, and the face of the older boy drifting in and out of the sun, like an eclipse, as he flailed at me.

With one finger I flick the cigarette away into the wind, then get back in the car. I check my watch. Visiting hours start in fifteen minutes. I put the car in drive and turn onto the hospital access road. I make my way slowly, tires crunching over the sand laid down by the pickup truck. The driver of the truck sees me coming and pulls over to let me pass.

I follow the signs to the main entrance, park the car, and go inside through an automatic door. The door slides closed behind me with a hiss, shutting out the wind and snow. The entryway is still, quiet, and shockingly warm. A guard in a dark blue uniform sits at a desk behind a thick plate of glass, eyeing me without much interest.

I approach the guard and tell him, through the speaker in the glass, that I am here to visit my brother.

He's a patient here? the guard asks.

Yes, I say.

Name?

I tell him my brother's name. He nods and places a clipboard and a pen in a sliding drawer on his side of the glass, then pushes the drawer through.

Fill that out, he says. He looks at the clock behind him. You can't come in for another ten minutes.

I nod and sit in one of the chairs lined up against the wall. The paperwork on the clipboard asks for my personal information, relationship to the patient, and reason for visit. There is also a disclaimer freeing the hospital of any liability if I am injured or killed. I smile to myself as I sign this in triplicate.

I bring the clipboard and the pen back to the desk and slide them through the drawer to the guard. He takes the clipboard out and sets it aside without looking at it. The pen he leaves in the drawer. I shove my hands into my pants pockets and cough a little.

Two minutes, the guard says without looking up.

I remember the high electric whine of a thousand grasshoppers. The taste of dirt and blood mingling in my mouth.

I wait the two minutes. When they have passed, the guard reaches under his desk and presses a switch hidden from my view. A loud electric buzzing sounds in the door on my right. The guard motions for me to open the door, which I do. I stand on the threshold, holding the door to keep it from closing and locking again, while the guard tells me where to go. When he has finished, I pass through.

Follow the corridor all the way down, he said. On this level the patients are allowed to move about freely. Some of them may talk to you, may even say something nasty or threatening. Just ignore them. Sure they smell bad and are strangely and sometimes only partially dressed. Some even look dangerous. Don't be fooled; they're harmless. All the same, keep walking. Don't stop for any reason. On the other hand, do not—I repeat, do *not*—run. When you reach the end of the corridor you'll find an elevator. Take this to the seventh floor. It will be dark in the elevator when the doors close, and it may seem rickety going up, but don't worry. If you're claustrophobic, keep it together; the ride to the seventh floor only lasts a few moments. When the elevator comes to a stop and the doors open, take a left and follow this corridor until you find the nurses' station. Don't worry about the patients here; on this level they're all locked in their rooms and supervised around the clock.

I follow the guard's instructions. At the nurses' station on the seventh floor a thin man in starched whites has me fill out more paperwork.

I remember my shirt tearing at the shoulder. A rock, half-exposed in the ground beneath me, jammed against the small of my back.

That's your brother? the man asks when I hand him the completed form.

Yes, I say.

Boy, has *he* been a handful, the man tells me. We've got only one orderly who can handle him. And he's out of work for at least a *week*.

Where is he? I ask, though I'm not really interested.

Yesterday we were taking your brother for a bath, the man says. We passed by the breakfast cart, and your brother took hold of one of those heavy plastic coffeepots and *smacked* Little John right in the chops with it. Broke his nose in *two places*.

The man laughs and shakes his head. I don't know what to say. So I say nothing.

I remember the tears coming, flowing. How I cried, afraid and ashamed, with a mouth full of blood and dirt, in the field under the hot sun, while a thousand grasshoppers buzzed in unison and the thin broken reeds and exposed rock pricked and stabbed.

*Any*way, the man says, motioning for me to follow him, that's why we're keeping your brother down here, in the *isolation room.* Danger to himself and others. We've had to dope him up pretty damn *good,* so don't expect him to carry on much of a conversation.

The man stops in front of the last door at the end of the hallway. The door is solid and windowless except for a small sliding partition at eye level. The man raps on the door three times with his knuckles, then calls to my brother and announces that he has a visitor. He slides a key into the keyhole and gives it two full turns. The tumblers roll inside the lock with a heavy metallic crack that resonates in the corridor, and then the door is open.

Go on, the man says to me. Don't worry. He's in restraints, and I'll be watching. The man slides the partition open to let me know what he means.

I think to tell him that I'm not worried. That despite the things my brother has done, despite the obvious fact that he's gone horribly and irretrievably insane, he is still, after all, my brother. But I realize that like everyone else, this man would not understand, and so I only nod and step through the door and listen as it closes behind me.

I remember my brother's silhouette rising behind the boy, blotting out the sun, huge and furious, like some vengeful god come to save me. I remember, suddenly, the words he repeated, over and over, as he beat the boy: *I am the one who kills and gives life! No one delivers from my power!*

But now, in here with my brother, somehow it doesn't matter to me anymore whether this is real memory or only imagined. I am suddenly hot and exhausted, and none of it matters a bit.

Then there is the other thing I came here for, and it seems best that I get it over with, before I lose what's left of my energy and resolve.

I put a hand in my jacket pocket, feel the hard weight there.

I've brought something for you, I say to my brother. I do not smile when I say this.

I pull my hand out, and the blackjack along with it. I hear the nurse behind me, on the other side of the locked door. He makes a sound like someone has punched him in the stomach. He bangs on the door, but I pay him no attention. I hear frantic muttering, and the jangle of keys in hands clumsy with panic, but by then he is much too late.

Retreat

Thus will I make mount Seir most desolate, and cut off from it him that passeth out and him that returneth. And I will fill his mountains with his slain men: in thy hills, and in thy valleys, and in all thy rivers, shall they fall that are slain with the sword. I will make thee perpetual desolations, and thy cities shall not return: and ye shall know that I am the Lord.

—Ezekiel 35:7–9

Arnold was not discharged from the Marines, honorably or otherwise; there was no time for anything so official, no time for paperwork or ceremony, with incessant artillery bombardments and people, military and civilian alike, turning on one another in their desperation to escape. His departure from the Marines could most accurately be described as an expulsion. He simply dropped his rifle, ditched his uniform, and fled Mexico City, scrabbling over crumbled brick and broken glass on a night lit bright as day by fire. He had no thought of the penalties for desertion, because there clearly would be none. In the face of the final, overwhelming Evolutionary Psychologist assault, all pretense of cohesion and command had been abandoned. Arnold had witnessed a lieutenant general strip naked in the middle of the street and don bloodstained clothes stolen from a corpse, his furtive, frightened expression decidedly unbecoming an officer, and soon after Arnold removed his own field utilities and headed north, toward a home he hadn't seen in eight years.

The going was tough. The roads were clogged with stalled and burned-out vehicles, belongings sacrificed for the sake of speed, rural Mexicans driving hogs and trailing children, and the ubiquitous dead and dying. Arnold limped along the shoulder, a chunk of shrapnel lodged deep in the meat of his thigh, spurred on through pain and thirst and despair not by fear of dying, but by fear of dying without seeing his mother again. Selia, his mother, who had cursed him when she'd learned of his plans to join the Postmodern Anthropologist Marines. Who had spit on her own kitchen floor as Arnold hugged his father and hoisted his bags to leave. And who, Arnold had learned from his father's letters, now was suffering from the same dementia that had killed her own mother.

Losing people should be sudden, Arnie, his father's most recent letter had read. *It's never easy no matter what the circumstances, but having it drag on and on is just unreasonable. There should be a moment, and when that moment's gone, the person should be, too. Then those left behind should be allowed to go through whatever they need to go through. Grief is hard enough without being harassed by living ghosts. But I'm losing your mother in bits and pieces, one memory at a time.*

This news had been particularly troubling to Arnold, not just because his mother was unwell, but because during the eight years he'd been in Mexico his own memory, previously near photographic, had slowly begun to flag. First he'd found himself unable to conjure up the faces of people from home. He would sit with his eyes closed and think of his mother, for example, would concentrate on the sweet chamomile scent of the natural perfume she wore, or the timbre of her ready laugh, but any image of her refused to rise. He tried other people—his father, friends, former teachers—and at best was able to produce only a murky, indistinct portrait in his mind, like something viewed underwater with the naked eye.

What made this all the more distressing was that, because he was a Marine interrogator, memory—both his and that of the Evo-Psych POWs he interviewed—was Arnold's stock-in-trade. For him to succeed in his job he needed to remember not just clearly but quickly, to be able to access a mental transcript of interviews with a particular subject and compare answers to similar questions from days and sometimes weeks earlier, to adjust his line of questioning on the fly and ferret out the truth. But as time went by and his memories of the distant past faded—how old had he been when his family had moved to the island? and what was the name of that girl he'd been so obsessed with in high school?—whatever was ailing him began to devour the information stored in his short-term banks, and despite the fact that he began recording interviews as a hedge against his suddenly spotty recall, he became useless as an interrogator.

Not that it mattered much; by this time the Evo-Psych block-ade had strangled and finally snuffed out the Marines' ability to fight. No food, no fuel, no ammo, no chance. The war was lost; this was as plain and inevitable as death, and no amount of reli-able, timely intel was going to change the fact. So Arnold fled, along with everyone else, and he imagined he had the same thing in mind as the other refugees: to reach home before the Evo-Psych troops poured north out of Mexico and laid waste to everything like a swarm of locusts.

As he limped further from Mexico City the number of those actively fleeing diminished, and with the sunrise the ranks of the dead swelled until the road was made nearly impassable by corpses. Hundreds, perhaps thousands of people, but animals too, dogs and goats and chickens and even an armadillo, squashed flat and crisping at its edges under the desert sun. For a while he was forced to the road's shoulder, but even there the bodies began piling up, and eventually he had no choice but to climb over them, grasping at feet, arms, and necks as though they were handholds on a steep mountain trail.

It was exhausting work, scaling corpses. To distract himself from the fatigue, the thirst and hunger, the sharp flare of pain that occurred each time he moved his leg, Arnold thought of his mother. First he tried, with the usual lack of success, to picture her in his mind's eye. Then he concentrated on willing her lu-cid, so that when he arrived home she would be who she always had been, not some bewildered stranger who merely looked like his mother, and she would hear what he had to say.

Because it was not a joyous and tearful reunion he had planned. Arnold still loved her, but time and distance had trans-formed that love into something remote and abstract, whereas the anger he had for her was real and immediate and had only grown in the years since he'd joined the Marines. He was no longer a sensitive teenager who bit his tongue to avoid incurring her wrath, but a man who could fall into a profound and untroubled sleep twenty minutes after tearing out a subject's fingernails or forcing him to eat hooks of broken glass. A man, in short, who expected to be on equal terms with the people in his life.

But he was beginning to doubt he'd have a chance to settle scores with his mother. As midday approached and the sun climbed high and hot, his legs gave out and he collapsed near the crest of a hill of bodies. It took a solid minute of effort for him to roll onto his back. Panting, he rested his head on the mange-pocked haunch of a dead goat and threw one arm over his eyes to block the sun. He fought to summon the mental strength to power his failing muscles. A few years earlier, when he'd still believed in the primacy of will and other tenets of Postmodern Anthropology, he would have been able to struggle to his feet on faith alone. Now his belief was as broken and scattered as Mexico City's defenses. No food, no water, no faith, no chance.

Arnold had moved far enough from the fighting that he no longer could hear the thunder of bombs and mortars, and the desert morning had been silent except for the occasional celebratory screech of vultures. But after he'd been lying atop the corpses long enough to develop aches from all the sharp angles beneath him, the knees and elbows and claws and hooves, he became aware of a distant rumbling, so faint at first that he couldn't be sure he was hearing it, then growing louder by increments as whatever was causing the sound slowly approached. Eventually he made out the whistling clatter of tank tracks, and he opened his eyes and saw an armored combat earthmover, which was really just a Schwarzkopf battle tank with a plow mounted on the front, moving toward him down the middle of the road. Bodies rode up the face of the plow and spilled off to the side, tumbling over one another like clothes in a dryer, stiff limbs flailing. Arnold raised an arm and waved weakly, and the tank stopped twenty feet from him, its turbine engine idling.

Under other circumstances, Arnold might have been more surprised than he was to see Crispy emerge from the turret. If he'd been in sharper mental condition, for example, or if Crispy hadn't had a well-deserved reputation as the sort of batshit lunatic who would steal a Schwarzkopf for a getaway vehicle without ever having driven one before. As it was, though, Arnold registered only a mild, fleeting incredulity as Crispy climbed down the front of the tank and scrambled over the mass of corpses to where he lay.

"Arnie," Crispy said, slinging one of Arnold's arms over his shoulders and lifting him, "I want you to know I'm making a noteworthy exception, here, to my current policy of running over everyone I see."

It took a moment for Arnold to unstick his tongue from the roof of his mouth. "I'm honored," he said finally. "Though if you don't have any water, I'd rather you just ran me over, too."

"Not to worry, not to worry," Crispy said. He heaved Arnold half onto the tank, then crouched and pushed with his hands on Arnold's behind. "Get on up there," he said, and Arnold, with some reluctance, kicked his feet until they found purchase. With the help of Crispy's boost, he flung himself up onto the turret. He found himself staring down the open hatch. Half a dozen sets of eyes stared back. Somehow Crispy had managed to cram three dogs, a pig, a goat, and his own pet, a thick-billed parrot he called Pepe, into the tank's interior.

"What's with the animals?" he said as Crispy clamored up beside him.

"You know me," Crispy said. "Not much for people, but I love me some critters."

Arnold did know him, well enough to have given him his nickname, which was a reference to Crispy's exclusive reliance on matches, cigarettes, and in extreme cases, hot irons and lighter fluid to extract information from subjects.

"Should I ask how you got the tank?" Arnold said.

"Probably not," Crispy said.

"How about the water?"

Crispy shook his head. "You don't wanna know. It just gets more gruesome."

"I meant, can I have some water?"

"Oh, yeah, yeah, of course." Crispy disappeared into the hatch, emerging a moment later with a plastic gallon jug, still sealed. "You'll have to ride up here," he said. "Not a whole lotta room down below."

Arnold opened the jug and drank fast, gulping, the water spilling over his chin and down his neck, soaking his shirt.

"Hey," Crispy called from inside the tank. "Don't waste it. I like you, Arnie, but don't waste my water."

The goat bleated once, as if to emphasize Crispy's words and the threat lurking behind them. Arnold wiped his mouth with the back of his hand. He capped the jug and handed it down through the hatch.

"Hold on," Crispy said. "I still don't really know how to drive this beast."

The tank lurched forward. Arnold nearly went tumbling over the back, but caught himself with a blind grasp at the lip of the hatch. As the turbines wound up and bodies began tumbling again, he tried to find a position comfortable enough for him to doze.

They rolled steadily north through the afternoon, gaining speed as they finally started to outpace the dead. Crispy stopped once to hack an arm from a corpse for the dogs ("They're eyeballing that goat like he's a ham sandwich") and a second time to pick up a tortoise sunning itself in the roadway. Though the pace was still slow, and though he was wary of Crispy, whose insanity was no longer held in check by military discipline and sanctioned opportunities to exercise his sadistic streak, Arnold was more optimistic with each passing mile. It wouldn't be long before they reached Texas, where he could say good-bye to Crispy and make his own way home.

His optimism was dampened a bit when dusk fell and Crispy brought the tank to a stuttering halt and handed the animals one by one up to him.

"We'll stay here tonight," Crispy said, pulling himself through the hatch. "Get an early start in the morning."

Arnold said nothing in protest, despite the fact that he suspected the more time he spent with Crispy, the more likely it was that something bad would happen, something that would keep him from home and the reckoning with his mother. If Crispy said they were staying overnight, that was that. It seemed wise not to do anything that would jeopardize his precarious favor with Crispy and hasten along that bad something.

He was so concerned with keeping Crispy happy, in fact, that despite his wound he tried to help in collecting loose sticks and scrub brush for a fire.

"Take a load off, Arnie," Crispy said to him. "Go drink some more water. You're weak as a kitten. I think I can manage a fire by myself."

Crispy could, of course, manage by himself, for which Arnold was grateful, because by the time the fire was going a breeze had already blown the day's heat out toward the mountains, and it was colder than Arnold could have imagined a few hours earlier. The chill reminded him of home, but again the memory was distant, intangible, as though he'd only read about Maine's frigid winters rather than experiencing more than a dozen firsthand. The animals, who (with the exception of the tortoise) had scattered upon being released from the tank, now straggled back in, drawn by the warmth and light.

Crispy sat cross-legged in the dirt, using his Ka-bar to roast strips of meat. The dogs lay near him, spellbound by the meat as it turned and sizzled at the point of the knife. When he was offered a piece Arnold didn't ask what it was; he was too hungry to let Crispy, certified animal-lover, misanthrope, and psychopath, confirm what he suspected.

"So where are you heading?" Crispy asked around a mouthful.

"Home," Arnold said. "North. Way, way north. Much further north than you'd ever want to go."

"I don't know about that," Crispy said. "I've got no real agenda, geographically speaking. No home to go to. I just want to get across the border so I can stop being crazy."

Arnold, perplexed, said nothing.

"What," Crispy said, gnawing another chunk of meat from the blade of the Ka-bar, "you think I don't know I'm crazy? It's not true, what they say. When you're nuts, you know. And there's no getting away from it. Crazy, morning, noon, and night. Crazy, crazy, crazy. Crazy dreams, even. But not for much longer."

"I don't understand," Arnold said.

"Hey," Crispy said, "don't humor me, Arnie. Okay? Don't act like it never occurred to you I might be a few sandwiches short of a picnic."

"That's not it, Crispy—"

"And don't get up on your high horse, either, superguy. 'Cause I've seen you do things that would qualify you for the bughouse, don't forget."

The difference being, Arnold thought, that he'd carried out his duties as an interrogator with the grim determination of a true believer, taking no pleasure in it, while Crispy regularly sported a rock-hard erection when putting matches out in subjects' eyes or applying flame to the soles of their feet, and made no effort to hide it.

"I know what you're thinking," Crispy said. "You're thinking there's a difference—you were just being a good soldier, and I would have done it for free—shit, I would have paid for the privilege." He tossed a bit of gristle to the dogs and threaded another strip onto the knife. "Well, you're right about one part. But answer this: How'd you sleep after your first interview?"

"I didn't," Arnold said. "For two days."

"Exactly. And how do you sleep now? Like a dead baby, am I right?" Crispy smiled at him over the flames. "Would your mama recognize the boy she sent off to war, Arnie?"

Arnold wasn't sure what made him angrier: that Crispy had a point, or that he'd brought Arnold's mother into it. "Would your mama recognize the depraved cocksucker she spawned?" he asked.

"Whoooooo, yeah!" Crispy laughed. "That's what I'm saying, right there. Picking a fight with a crazy man." He checked the meat for doneness, tore it in two, and handed half to Arnold. "We're not all that different, you and I."

"That wasn't what I was talking about, anyway," Arnold said. "If you'd let me get a word in edgewise."

"Whatcha mean?"

"I know you're fucking crackers, Crispy. What I meant was I don't understand how getting north of the border will suddenly change that fact."

Crispy studied him, as if trying to determine whether he was serious. "You don't know?"

"Know what?"

"How long have you been with this outfit, anyway?"

"Eight years."

"Don't you talk with anyone back home?"

"My parents live on an island by themselves," Arnold said. "They're a bit out of touch."

"Well shit, hombre," Crispy said, "one word, two syllables: nanotech."

"That's three syllables," Arnold said.

"Whatever. I'm talking robots the size of an atom. Pro-grammed to cure whatever ails you. You got cancer, they find the tumor and kill it off. Got a bad memory you wish you didn't, they sniff out the brain cells that house it and wipe 'em clean. And if you're crazy, they just make little adjustments—patch up a bad DNA strand, scrub the neurotransmitters clean—along with any required memory purging. And presto-chango. The potential applications are pretty much infinite, but you get the idea."

Arnold laughed. "You're crazier than I thought."

"That's what your mouth says. But your eyes say something else. You're intrigued. You're thinking about all the things you'd like to fix. And why not? *You'd* be crazy not to."

Arnold said nothing for a moment. Then he asked, "Can they restore memories, too?"

"Don't know," Crispy said. "I'm not an expert. But you don't have to know how it works to know that it does."

Crispy wiped the knife clean on his pantleg, sheathed it, and lay down on his side in the dirt. "Listen, it goes without saying that it's been a long day. I'm going to sleep. So don't talk anymore, all right?"

Within two minutes, Crispy was snoring. The dogs, realizing no more handouts were forthcoming, laid their heads on their paws and closed their eyes. Arnold fashioned a crude pillow with his boots. His mind, exhausted to the point of mania, gnawed at the edges of this nanotech idea, and he had just enough time to think there was no way he'd get to sleep before he passed out cold.

Crispy kicked him awake sometime before sunrise. "Rise and shine, amigo," he said. He was wide-eyed, smiling nervously. "Can you hear the explosions? Those Evo-Psych fuckers are moving fast."

Arnold turned an ear to the south and listened. He heard nothing but sagebrush rustling in the breeze.

Crispy was loading the animals into the tank. "Have you seen the goat?" he asked.

"I haven't seen anything. I've been asleep the whole time."

Crispy eyed him. "You sure about that?"

Wary, Arnold kept his exasperation in check. "I have no idea where the goat is," he said evenly.

"Little guy wandered off," Crispy said. He climbed the side of the tank and lowered himself into the hatch. "Oh well. No time. Let's get a move on."

Crispy had the tank rolling even before Arnold could scramble to his position atop the turret. They hurtled along the road for hours without slowing or stopping. Turbines screaming, the tank kicked and listed; Arnold's hands grew numb from clutching the lip of the hatch to avoid being bucked off.

By late afternoon they'd reached the Solidaridad Colombia bridge and found it destroyed. Nothing remained but the bridge's concrete supports, cut to half their original height by an explosion and jutting up from the waters of the Rio Grande like broken stalagmites. Across the river the Texas border town of Boca Buitre was visible, all squat dun-colored buildings and dirt streets.

"Dammit," Crispy said, climbing out of the tank. "Who blew up the bridge?"

"There's a sign," Arnold said, pointing.

And there was. A large white placard had been driven into the earth on the edge of the riverbank, bearing the same message in English, Spanish, Vietnamese, and Chinese.

Dear Evolutionary Psychologists
and Other Concerned Parties:

Please accept our sincere apologies for this war and its attendant destruction, loss of life, and general unhappiness. As a nation we have decided, albeit belatedly, that all this philosophical bickering is quite silly. We have therefore resolved to end our part in the conflict and to take broad, clinically proven measures to forget that it

happened in the first place. By the same token, we put our trust in the benevolent nature of your great people and ask that you not invade our country and raze our cities and slaughter our families. Again, please accept our sincere apologies and best wishes.

—The Government and Citizens of the United States

"What the *fuck*?" Crispy said.

"Indeed," Arnold said. "Precisely what I was thinking."

Crispy threw a haymaker at the air. "How the fuck are we going to get across?"

"Hey, relax," Arnold said. "We'll figure it out."

Crispy seized him by the shirt. "Don't tell me to relax," he said. "You heard the bombs this morning. They're *right behind us*. We don't have time for this."

"Okay." Arnold raised his hands in appeasement. "Okay. It looks like we're going swimming, then."

Crispy released him with a shove. "No," he said. "No way. The animals. We're taking the tank."

"What? The tank will sink, Crispy."

"It's not that deep. You can see rocks sticking up. There. And there."

Those "rocks," Arnold noted, were actually the broken remnants of the bridge, and there was no telling how deeply they were piled up under the surface of the water. Still, Crispy was frantic and dangerous, so he said nothing.

Crispy climbed back into the tank. "Get on, if you're coming," he said.

Arnold didn't like this, but he liked his chances of swimming across with a bum leg even less. He clambered up to the turret as Crispy pushed the tank forward and over the bank. As they approached the river Arnold could see a shelf of rock just under the surface, extending maybe thirty feet from the river's edge, and beyond that nothing was visible in the dark water.

On the floor of the bank they hit a lip of level ground at such an extreme angle that the plow ripped up a chunk of earth the size of a Volkswagen. The tank bucked mightily and splashed into the river, driving foamy brownish waves before it. On the rock shelf the water rose only to the middle of the tracks.

"See?" Crispy hollered up at him. "Ha! I told you it wasn't deep!"

Emboldened, Crispy jammed the accelerator forward. Arnold crouched on the balls of his feet, ready to leap.

At the shelf's edge the tank paused, pitched slowly forward with a deep mechanical groan, and sank like the sixty tons of steel that it was.

Arnold pushed off with his one good leg, but couldn't escape the water rushing into the vacuum behind the tank's descent. The sun disappeared. In the darkness, enveloped by a cloud of swirling bubbles, he lost all sense of which direction was up. He could hear the deep, muffled clatter of the tank's machinery still grinding away, but in the water the sound was diffuse, coming from every direction, and so was no help in determining where he needed to go to find his next breath.

He fought to calm himself as his lungs smoldered, then burst into flames. He grew still and waited, trusting that his natural buoyancy would tell him what his senses couldn't. After a moment he felt his body begin to drift in one direction, and when he was sure he began to claw and kick at the water, following this drift, certain that at any moment he would break the surface and find air, but it was taking much longer than he'd hoped or expected, and now starbursts performed little slow-motion explosions before his eyes and he became *too* calm. Suddenly, taking another breath seemed not so urgent after all, and even as he struggled to focus on getting out of this mess his mind drifted along with his body, turning to thoughts of his mother, and how was it possible to love and hate one person with equal intensity at the same time, he wondered, just as his head broke the surface and the reptilian portion of his brain demanded and got a deep lungful of air.

The oxygen hit him like a slap to the face, and the urgency returned. He looked around and saw that two of the dogs had come to the surface and were paddling for the bank on the Texas side of the river. Arnold tried to follow them, but the current was too strong for him to swim against with just one leg. He called to the dogs. They continued swimming away, so he called again, and this time one of them did a slow, wide semicircle and headed back.

The dog brushed against Arnold and allowed him to grab hold of its tail. Legs pumping, it did another semicircle and pointed its nose toward the shore, dragging him along. He tried to help by stroking with his free hand, but the dog was strong and seemingly tireless, and soon they were in Texas, soaked, exhausted, and alive.

Arnold lay on his back. "Good boy," he said to the dog, but it apparently felt no special bond had been established; already it had rejoined its companion, and together they trotted into Boca Buitre, sniffing and marking as they went, without so much as a glance back at him.

There was no sign of Crispy. The river had resumed its glassy, languid flow, with nothing to indicate that it had carried a man, a pig, a dog, a tortoise, a parrot, and a battle tank to their deaths only moments before. Arnold watched and waited. He wasn't sure if he hoped to see Crispy emerge or not, but he realized as the minutes passed that what he hoped for was irrelevant, and when he saw the lifeless body of Pepe the parrot bob to the surface, wings akimbo, he struggled to his feet and limped toward Boca Buitre.

He expected to find the town empty, as all the small desert communities they'd passed in Mexico had been, but to his surprise there were people about, mowing dead lawns, checking their mailboxes, lying in grease-stained driveways as they worked on old cars. Dripping wet and limping, he earned more than a few sidelong glances as he made his way to what passed as downtown: a four-way intersection with a general store on one corner.

Inside, Arnold took bags of chips and cookies, two cans of beef stew, and several bottles of water to the counter. A boy of twelve or so, slightly chubby, sun-freckled, sat at the register.

"I don't have any money," Arnold said.

"Then you can't have the food," the boy told him.

"I've just come from the war."

The boy stared at him silently, then turned on his stool and yelled through a doorway. "Carlene!"

A pear-shaped woman in a sunflower T-shirt emerged from the stockroom. She brushed a strand of hair from her forehead and smiled at Arnold. "What's going on, Ty?"

"This man doesn't want to pay for his food."

"I'm not trying to cause trouble," Arnold said. "I was telling your son—"

"Oh, Ty's not my son," the woman said, still smiling. "He's my nephew, near as I can remember. I'm pretty sure I had a sister, and Ty was her boy. But who can be certain about these things?" She laughed cheerily and rubbed brisk circles on Ty's back with the palm of her hand. "We've all forgotten so much, it seems."

"Well, I was telling your nephew that I've just come from the fighting in Mexico, and I don't have any money."

"There was a fight? You do look like you've been worked over pretty good."

"The war, miss," Arnold said. "I was with the PoMo Marines in Mexico for eight years."

"And on top of that, you're delirious. Did you take a hit on the head?" The woman came around the counter, still smiling, and put a hand on Arnold's arm. "You should go upstairs and lie down on our sofa for a while. Ty, take him up to the apartment."

Arnold wanted to protest—he was anxious to keep moving toward home—but the idea of napping on something softer than packed dirt was too appealing to pass up.

Ty stood up from the stool. "Come on," he said, disappearing through the doorway. Arnold followed him up a narrow set of stairs to an attic apartment full of hundreds of shipping boxes bearing labels such as INVISIBLE TUMMY TRIMMER and PEE-B-GONE COMPLETE URINE CLEANUP KIT. The boxes were stacked three and four deep, from floor to ceiling, leaving only a narrow walkway through the apartment.

"Carlene keeps saying she'll get rid of these," Ty told him. "But she won't. She's worried she'll need to return something and won't have a box to send it in. Here's the living room."

With all the boxes, Arnold had to squeeze past Ty to get to the sofa. He took off his boots and lay down.

"Thanks, Ty," Arnold said, his eyes closed. "Tell Carlene I said thank you. I'll just sleep a few hours and be on my way."

"She won't care how long you stay. She's cracked, like everyone else," Ty said. He pretended to study the label on a box, then asked, "You were in the Marines?"

Arnold opened his eyes and looked at him. "You remember the war?"

"I remember everything," Ty said. "When the men came I held the pills under my tongue. When they left, I spit them out." He scoffed at the simplicity of it, though clearly he was proud of his cunning.

"Does anyone else remember?"

"Not around here," Ty said. "Nobody I know."

Arnold considered. "Ty, I'm going to take a nap, and then you and I need to talk," he said. "About something bad. Something scary. You think you can do that?"

Ty scrunched up his face. "Whatever," he said. "I'm not afraid."

"Good," Arnold said. He lifted his hand to the boy. "My name's Arnold, by the way."

Ty shook his hand, once, then let it drop. "That's a geeky name," he said.

Arnold hid his amusement at this. "Better than Ty," he said. "Now let me sleep."

■

When Arnold woke the room was still bright with sunlight. For a moment he was disoriented—he felt like he'd been out longer than an hour—until he realized it was the next morning.

On the television a man was asking, "What if creating beautiful designer nails was as easy as writing your name?"

Arnold did not know the answer to this. Fortunately the man on the television did.

"Well, now it is!" he said. "With new Nail Dazzle Duo-Pen!"

Carlene squeezed her plump body through the boxes on either side of the doorway. "You're awake," she said. "For a while we thought you'd never wake up."

Arnold felt something tight on his leg where the shrapnel was lodged. He looked down and saw his thigh had been wrapped in gauze and white medical tape.

"Yeah, sorry," Carlene said. "You were bleeding on the sofa. That must have been some fight you were in! Obviously I didn't want to take your *pants* off"—here she tittered and covered her mouth with her hand—"so I just bandaged you as best I could."

"No, it's okay," Arnold said. He sat up and rubbed his eyes. "Thank you."

Carlene quickly changed the subject. "I've got some huevos rancheros going," she said. "It'll be just a few minutes. The remote's there on that box if you want to watch TV."

She disappeared into the kitchen again. Arnold flipped through the channels, trying to find the news, but there was nothing on except infomercials.

A man named Chef Henry told him about "a knife so sharp you can cut a pineapple in midair."

A woman asked if he was sick of feeling uncomfortable in his own body, and if he was ready to get serious about rock-hard abs.

Another woman informed him that the average person carried five to ten pounds of toxic matter in their intestines—but now there was a way for him to scrub his insides clean.

"Breakfast is ready!" Carlene called from the kitchen.

Arnold found a place set for him at the table. Ty sat flanked by columns of boxes, quietly forking eggs and salsa into his mouth. While Arnold and Ty ate, Carlene hovered at the gas range, fiddling aimlessly with pans and spice containers.

"How is it?" she asked when he was nearly finished.

"Very good," Arnold said.

"It used to take me an hour to make the salsa," she said. "But I got this Magic Bullet chopper-dicer thing, and now I'm done in five minutes. It's great."

"Sounds like a lifesaver," he said.

Carlene took off her apron. "I've got to get downstairs and open the store. I asked Ty here to take you to the doctor when you're ready."

"Terrific," Arnold said, though he had no intention of going. "Thanks so much, Carlene."

"You boys stay out of trouble." She winked at them and went down the stairs.

"So, Ty," Arnold said, wiping his mouth and pushing his plate away. "That thing I wanted to talk about."

"Yeah."

"I don't have time to sugarcoat it. Are you sure you're ready to hear this?"

"I'm not a kid," Ty said. "I take care of myself, basically."

Arnold studied the boy's face. "Okay," he said. "Here it is: We have to leave this place. Today. Or we're going to die."

"The war," Ty said.

"Yes, the war. We lost. They're coming to kill us. It's that simple."

"Carlene won't go."

"Why not?"

"None of them will," Ty said. "They won't listen. I told you, they're cracked. They don't remember anything. They'll say we're the crazy ones."

"Carlene must remember something, Ty. She knows she's your aunt, after all."

"She's not my aunt," Ty said. "She's my mother."

Arnold, who believed that eight years of combat had removed him permanently to a place beyond shock, was stunned.

"What about your father?" he asked.

"Dead. He was with the Marines, went to some place called Guam, and never came back," Ty said.

"She doesn't remember him at all?"

Ty plowed rows in the leftover salsa with his fork. "Sometimes she gets upset for no reason. I find her in the bedroom, looking out the window and crying. But not really crying. She's still smiling, but there are tears on her face. I ask her what's wrong. She says she doesn't know, don't worry, she just gets sad sometimes. Whatever."

"Ty," Arnold said, "we need to convince your mother to come with us."

"You can try, but it won't work."

"I think you care more than you're letting on," Arnold said. "And if you don't, you should."

Ty stared at him. "She'd rather forget my father than remember me," he said. "So, whatever."

The kid had a point. "All right," Arnold said. "I'll talk to Carlene. But I still need you to do something for me. Do you guys have a car?"

"Didn't you see the truck outside?"

"A truck, okay, that's good. I want you to go downstairs and tell Carlene to come up here. Tell her you'll watch the store."

"Okay."

"I need you to pull the truck around front to the pumps—you can drive, right?—and fill it up. Then pack it with food and water from the store."

"I can drive."

"Good," Arnold said. "Go ahead. We'll be down soon."

Ty went downstairs. While he waited, Arnold thought he heard the radio-static sound of a jet flying high overhead. He threw open the kitchen window, leaned out and looked up, and though the sky was high and clear he could see no vapor trail.

If he hadn't known better, he would have chalked it up to imagination.

Carlene entered the kitchen, beaming her sweet, half-vacant smile. "Ty said you wanted to see me?"

"Yeah," Arnold said. "Let's have a seat. I want to ask you a few questions, if you don't mind."

They sat opposite each other at the kitchen table.

"Do you remember your husband, Carlene?" Arnold asked.

Her smile widened. "I've never been married."

"Sure you have. Your husband was killed in the war."

"Poor thing," she said. "You really aren't well. We have to get you to the doctor."

"Carlene," Arnold said, "I think there's still a part of you that knows what I'm saying is true."

Carlene stood up from the table. Still smiling, she said, "I think I'll go into the living room and watch some TV."

Arnold followed her at a distance, waiting as she squeezed herself between the boxes, reclined on the sofa, and pointed the remote control at the television set. Over the voice of a woman outlining the virtues of the RoboMower, Arnold heard again the sound of jet engines above, louder and unmistakable this time.

"Look at me, Carlene," he said. "You know you had a husband. You know Ty is your son."

Though her smile remained, Carlene's eyes began to shimmer. "I could really use one of these," she said, pointing at the television. "Those weeds out back just grow and grow, and I never have time to trim them down."

"Carlene, please, listen to me," Arnold said. "Men are coming to kill us. We have to leave now."

"No, I think I'll stay," Carlene said. "You boys go ahead and have fun."

Arnold reached out and grasped her wrist. "We don't have time to argue," he said.

Carlene leaned up, and for a moment Arnold thought she would come along quietly, neither yielding nor resisting. But then she bit him, hard enough to tear the flesh away from his knuckles. He pulled back, and she lay down again, her smile stained now with a streak of red.

The sound of distant explosions rattled the building. The television went dead, cutting off a man in the middle of his explanation of the many uses for Odor Assassin.

"Oh, a thunderstorm," Carlene said. "We haven't had a thunderstorm in a long time. It hardly ever rains here, but it's so nice when it does."

Clutching his hand to his chest, Arnold watched Carlene curl slowly into a ball with her fists tucked under her bloody chin. She was still smiling, still staring at the blank and silent television, and Arnold felt a sudden, abiding sadness—not for her, but for Ty, and not for the fact that Ty would soon lose his mother, but for the way in which he already had.

Another series of explosions shook the floor beneath Arnold's feet, and he turned away from Carlene, running through the kitchen and down the stairs. Outside he found the truck idling near the pumps. Ty sat in the passenger seat, watching calmly through the windshield as columns of black smoke rose from a dozen fires all over town.

Arnold got in on the driver's side.

"I told you," Ty said, still watching the sky.

"I know," Arnold said. He put the truck in gear and pointed it west rather than north, driving through the bombs and the fire and the people in the streets who didn't seem to notice their world was being destroyed, and even when Boca Buitre had dropped below the horizon and Ty began to cry like an old man, quietly, his body still, neither of them said another word.

Acknowledgments

Normally I find words to be more than equal to the task at hand. As a means of thanking the people who contributed to the writing of this book, however, words are woefully inadequate. But since my cooking skills have eroded and I can't legally offer free medical services, it seems words will have to do:

Big thanks to the undisputed heavyweight champion of literary agents, Simon Lipskar, a tireless advocate who daily, or at least biweekly, pulls off the improbable feat of making me feel like his only client. Also to Nikki Furrer, Dan Lazar, and everyone at Writers House for putting up with me/covering my butt.

Big thanks to my editor, Molly Stern, who was kind enough to lead me by the hand to a better book when she probably wanted to whack me with a cattle prod to expedite the process. Also to Alessandra Lusardi, Laura Tisdel, and the other behind-the-scenes folks at Viking. You won't see their names on the dust jacket, but they can rightly claim the bigger slice of credit for any success I enjoy.

Thanks to all my talented and supportive compadres at the